Just for the Summer

Just for the Summer

Alaina Robbins

Contents

This book is dedicated to my grandparents, without whom my summers in Tahoe would be non-existent. Therefore, this book would not have been possible. Thank you for everything you've done for me.

First Printing, 2025

1

Rachel

If I'd known returning to Lake Tahoe meant facing Adam Harrison again, I might have thought twice about this summer plan.

Six years ago

The sun was setting over the lake, casting a warm glow over the backyard where my friends and family were gathered, laughing and talking. My mom had hung fairy lights around the patio, and the soft light made everything feel almost magical. I should have been having the perfect birthday—except that Adam Harrison was here, somehow managing to ruin it.

I caught him leaning against the picnic table, smirking as he watched me try to carry a giant bowl of chips without dropping it.

“Need a hand, birthday girl?” he called out, too loud, just as I stumbled. A few people turned to look, and I felt my cheeks burn.

“Nope, I’ve got it,” I replied through clenched teeth, setting the bowl down on the table a little harder than necessary. Adam strolled over anyway, casually popping a chip into his mouth like he belonged there, which he definitely didn’t.

“Sixteen now, huh?” He grinned, eyes twinkling with that annoyingly familiar look that meant he was about to say something obnoxious. “You sure you’re old enough for the big-kid parties?”

I rolled my eyes. “Funny, coming from someone who still thinks scaring people with fake spiders is hilarious.”

“Oh, come on, Turner,” he said, taking a chip and crunching it loudly. “You’ve gotta admit, watching you scream was pretty priceless.”

“Yeah, well, I’m sure that’ll be the high point of your year,” I shot back, crossing my arms. “Why are you even here, anyway?”

He shrugged, pretending to look thoughtful. “Hmm, let’s see... free food, and I get to tease you. Win-win.”

I glared at him, but he just laughed, unfazed. He'd always had that irritating ability to get under my skin and somehow enjoy every second of it.

"You could at least pretend to be a decent person for, like, one hour," I said, exasperated.

He leaned in, lowering his voice. "Where's the fun in that?"

With that, he sauntered off, leaving me fuming and wishing I hadn't invited half the neighborhood—including him.

Present Day

The familiar curve of the winding Tahoe road came into view as I maneuvered my car around the last bend, through the tunnel into the familiar Tahoe I'd always loved. The trees parted to reveal a sparkling slice of blue lake in the distance. Six years since I'd been back here, and yet it looked exactly the same—like the lake and the mountains had waited just for me, untouched by time.

The water shimmered, the sun's rays bouncing off the rippling waves. The water changed from shades of aqua to deep blue as the lake stretched on endlessly. Geese roamed the beaches, searching for unattended food to steal. The lake was dotted with a canvas of both locals and tourists. Swimmers, people paddle boarding, parasailers, boats, and jetskis. I had forgotten just how much Tahoe felt like home.

The driveway to our family cabin was shaded by tall pines, their scent filling the warm summer air. Pinecones were scattered throughout the drive, and the front lawn was covered in dark green grass. I couldn't help but be taken back to the memories we had, playing on the lawn as kids. We had water balloon fights, played volleyball, and even peeled corn husks for dinner on the overgrown grass. It was the same cabin my grandma had spent her summers in as a child. I parked and sat for a moment, taking it in. The cabin stood just as I remembered, nestled between the trees, the front porch slightly weathered but still welcoming. Memories tugged at the edges of my mind: late-night laughter with friends, marshmallow-sticky fingers, sunset walks on the beach, endless summer days spent swimming and exploring.

I grabbed my bag from the passenger seat and climbed out of the car, stretching as I breathed in the crisp mountain air. The thought of a whole summer here—away from city noise, final exams, and the chaos of life after college—felt like a dream I could finally hold in my hands. And yet, something nagged at me. A feeling I couldn't quite shake, as if I were stepping back into an old life that didn't fit quite right anymore.

I stepped onto the porch and fumbled for the spare key hidden beneath a basket of pinecones, a relic of my dad's "better safe than sorry" approach to life. Pushing the door open, I was greeted by the comforting smell of cedar and the sight of our cozy, mismatched furniture. I dropped my bag onto the couch and exhaled, feeling a little of the tension I'd carried melt away.

I was home.

I walked through the small cabin, my fingertips trailing over familiar surfaces. The cabin was modest and hadn't been redecorated for a few decades. It was just how I remembered it from my childhood, and it was perfect. In the kitchen, my mom had left a note on the fridge, probably from her last visit: *Remember to air out the blankets and don't forget to feed the chipmunks.* I smiled to myself, wondering if the chipmunks had missed me too.

I opened the back door and stepped onto the deck, taking in the breathtaking view of the lake just a short walk down the hill. Sunlight danced across the water, casting sparkles that made everything look like a postcard. The only thing missing was the sound of laughter, the thrill of a dozen people crowded around in swim trunks and flip-flops. It was peaceful—but a little lonely.

As I took it all in, I heard the unmistakable rumble of an engine coming up the gravel drive next door. A sudden, sharp memory hit me, and I almost laughed out loud. Of course. I should've known I wouldn't be entirely alone out here.

Before I could duck back inside, a truck pulled into the driveway next door. And there he was: Adam Harrison, leaning out of the driver's side window, his gaze already fixed on me with that infuriating half-smirk I remembered far too well.

"Hey, Turner" he called out, that same teasing lilt in his voice. "Didn't think you'd be brave enough to come back here after all this time."

I crossed my arms, unable to keep from smiling as I called back, "And I see you're still here, terrorizing the neighborhood."

He laughed, the sound carrying across the pines. "Guess some things never change."

I rolled my eyes and turned back toward the cabin, heart pounding a little faster than I'd like to admit. Apparently, I hadn't left every part of my past behind in Tahoe.

* * *

I'd just finished unpacking when the sound of tires crunching on gravel announced the arrival of my sister, Sarah, and her boyfriend, Kyle. I walked to the front porch, grinning as I watched Sarah climb out of the passenger seat with her usual burst of energy. She spotted me and waved excitedly.

"Rachel!" she shouted, bounding up the steps with her arms wide open. I barely had time to brace myself before she threw herself at me, wrapping me in a tight hug.

"Hey, kiddo," I laughed, hugging her back. "Missed you."

"I can't believe we're finally doing this!" she squealed, pulling away to look at me with her usual bright smile. "A whole summer together, just us—well, plus Kyle, but I figured you wouldn't mind."

Kyle was getting their bags from the trunk, giving me a wave and a smile as he walked up to the porch. "Hey, Rachel. Thanks for letting me crash your girls' summer," he said with a warm grin.

"No problem, Kyle. You're family, too." I gave him a quick hug and took one of the bags from his hands. "Come on, let me show you guys your room."

Sarah took my arm as we headed inside. "This place is exactly how I remembered it. It's like stepping into a time capsule," she said, looking around with a nostalgic smile. "You have no idea how excited I was when you said we could do this. I know I was too young to come for the 'big kid' summers, but this is finally my year!"

I laughed. "Well, you're here now, and we've got a lot of lost summers to make up for."

I led them down the hallway to the guest bedroom, which my parents had freshly painted the last time they'd been here. I could tell Sarah was thrilled by the little touches—fresh linens, a stack of our old board games, a vase of wildflowers she'd definitely attribute to my mom's doing.

Kyle set their bags down, glancing around the room. "This is great, Rachel. Thanks again."

"No problem at all." I glanced back toward the front windows, the lake visible in the distance. "We're in for a good summer. You guys hungry? I was thinking about firing up the grill for dinner tonight."

Sarah's eyes lit up. "Yes! Let's do it. And I brought stuff for s'mores. You can't have a proper Lake Tahoe summer without them."

We made our way back to the kitchen, catching up as I gathered everything we'd need for grilling. I'd barely finished setting up when I heard another sound—this time, footsteps crunching up the gravel path to the front porch. My stomach did a little flip as I looked up.

Adam was leaning against the porch railing, looking far too comfortable as he took in the scene.

"Well, look who's got company," he said, flashing a smirk in my direction.

Sarah turned, her eyes widening a little as she noticed Adam. I could practically see her curiosity flickering to life, her gaze darting between the two of us.

"Oh, hey there," she said, clearly trying to play it cool. "I'm Sarah, Rachel's sister. Well... step-sister."

Adam nodded, giving her a friendly smile. "Adam. Neighbor. Lake Tahoe local—unfortunately for your sister."

I rolled my eyes. "Unfortunately for everyone."

Sarah nudged me with her elbow, her eyes sparkling. "Oh, I like him," she whispered, just loud enough for me to hear. I shot her a warning look, but she just grinned wider.

Adam took a few steps forward. "So, are we just chatting out here, or is this an open invite for dinner?"

"Sure," I said, trying to sound casual. "Just don't expect me to save you the best piece."

He laughed, clearly undeterred. "Wouldn't dream of it."

As I fired up the grill and set out plates, I couldn't help but feel that the summer was already shaping up to be more complicated than I'd planned. With my sister's knowing glances, Kyle's easy-going presence, and Adam's maddening smirk from across the table, I had a feeling things were just getting started.

* * *

The scent of grilled food filled the air as we all sat down at the picnic table, plates piled high with burgers, grilled vegetables, and potato salad. The sun was dipping lower over the lake, casting a golden glow across the yard. It should have been a peaceful, relaxing dinner. And it would have been—if Adam hadn't been here, already getting under my skin.

"So, Turner," Adam began, a mischievous grin already forming on his face. "Tell us what college life is like for a small-town girl in the big, bad city. Do they still have to send you directions just to find your classes?"

I narrowed my eyes, taking a slow bite of my burger before answering. "It's funny, Adam. I thought people outgrew small-town jabs after high school, but I guess some things never change."

He laughed, clearly unfazed. "Hey, I'm just saying. The last time I saw you, you got lost on the hike to Echo Lake, and that was with a map."

I rolled my eyes, but Sarah perked up, clearly intrigued. "Wait, when did this happen?"

"Years ago," I said quickly, waving it off. "Adam's just trying to remind me that he's the 'big-shot local,' as if that's something impressive."

Adam leaned back, looking entirely too amused. "Oh, come on, Turner. Don't pretend you don't need my Tahoe expertise. It's cute, really. You'd be totally lost here without me."

I scoffed. "Right, because I've clearly been struggling all these years without your expert guidance."

Kyle chuckled, sensing the tension but probably not fully understanding the history behind it. "You two must have been close friends growing up," he said, glancing between us.

Adam smirked, his gaze flicking over to me. "Close friends? I think Turner would call it more of a 'necessary evil.'"

"Or just an evil," I muttered under my breath, reaching for the bowl of potato salad. But Sarah, always the troublemaker, jumped right in.

"So, what I'm hearing is… this is like a classic childhood frenemies situation," she said, giving me a grin that I did not appreciate. "You know, like a TV show where the girl and the annoying boy secretly have chemistry?"

I almost choked on my food. "No. Nope. That is absolutely not what this is."

Adam's smirk grew as he leaned forward, resting his elbows on the table. "Careful, Turner. Deny it too much, and people might get suspicious."

I glared at him, desperately trying to ignore the heat rising in my cheeks. "Believe me, Adam, no one here is getting any ideas."

"Good," he replied smoothly. "Wouldn't want anyone thinking you might actually like having me around."

I scoffed, feeling a flash of frustration—and maybe something else I didn't want to name. "Like is a strong word."

Adam chuckled, lifting his drink in a mock toast. "I'll take that as a compliment."

Sarah and Kyle exchanged amused glances, clearly enjoying the back-and-forth. Meanwhile, I was doing everything I could to keep my irritation in check, but Adam was making it nearly impossible.

I turned to Kyle, desperate to change the subject. "So, Kyle, are you planning to do any hiking while you're here? There are some gorgeous trails."

Adam couldn't resist chiming in. "Turner can probably recommend some good spots... if she remembers how to get there."

That was it. "I'm pretty sure I'll survive," I said, shooting him a look. "And if anyone's going to get lost, it'll be you, with that overinflated sense of direction."

Adam just laughed, holding up his hands in mock surrender. "Okay, okay. I'll back off—for now."

Dinner wrapped up with more laughter and teasing, mostly directed at me, thanks to Adam's relentless charm and Sarah's encouragement. And as much as he drove me crazy, I couldn't deny that a part of me—even if I'd never admit it—didn't mind the attention.

* * *

The night had fallen, and the air around Lake Tahoe was cool as Sarah, Kyle, and I strolled into one of the local bars, the kind of place that had a great view of the lake and a jukebox that seemed to play the same country songs every weekend. It was a classic Tahoe vibe—laid-back, casual, and perfect for a night out after a day of settling into the cabin.

We found a table near the bar, and I leaned back in my seat, letting the music and laughter of the crowd wash over me. I hadn't realized how much I missed the easy rhythm of this place, even if I wasn't exactly thrilled about being home.

Sarah, ever the social butterfly, immediately struck up a conversation with Kyle, and I found myself alone, nursing my drink and watching the crowd. That's when I saw him—a guy at the bar who was eyeing me from across the room, looking entirely too interested. My stomach twisted.

He was probably in his late twenties, wearing a button-down shirt that was too tight around his neck and a pair of jeans that looked like they hadn't seen the inside of a washing machine in weeks. His eyes lingered on me for a moment too long, and I looked away, hoping he would take the hint.

But he didn't.

In fact, he seemed to take that as an invitation to move closer. I felt a shiver of discomfort as he slid into the seat next to me, his breath heavy with the stale scent of beer.

"Hey there," he said with a grin that didn't quite reach his eyes. "You come here often?"

I forced a smile, trying to keep my voice steady. "Just visiting for the summer. Not really my scene, though."

"Oh, I'm sure I can make it more interesting," he said, leaning in too close. "You're way too pretty to be sitting alone."

I could already feel the red flags waving, but before I could come up with a polite excuse to leave, I saw him. Adam. He walked in with a few of his friends, his broad shoulders filling the doorway. He spotted me almost immediately, his eyes narrowing slightly before a slow smirk tugged at the corner of his mouth.

I looked back at the creepy guy, who was now trying to move even closer, and my patience snapped.

Without thinking, I stood up, grabbed my drink, and without a word, walked straight toward Adam. He hadn't seen me coming until I reached him, and before he could say a word, I stood on tiptoe and kissed him—hard, and with absolutely no warning.

The sound of Adam's friends hooting and calling out in surprise mixed with Sarah's laughter at our table. I pulled back just enough to look up at Adam, who was staring down at me with wide eyes, a mix of confusion and amusement on his face.

"There," I said, my voice louder than necessary, making sure the creepy guy and everyone else in the bar heard. "That should get him off my back."

I turned to Adam's friends, who were all grinning like they had front-row tickets to a show. "We're—uh—we're dating. Just wanted to make that clear."

Adam's eyes flickered to me, then to the guy who had been hovering over me. The creepy guy stood frozen in his seat, clearly thrown off by the sudden turn of events. I shot him one last look, making sure he got the message, and then I turned back to Adam, my heart racing.

"Yeah, we're *dating*," I repeated, a little louder this time, crossing my arms over my chest as I glared at him. "So if you could go away now, that'd be great."

The creepy guy finally seemed to take the hint. With a muttered curse, he slunk away from the bar, clearly deciding I wasn't worth the trouble. I watched him leave, and only then did I allow myself to breathe again.

I turned back to Adam, who was still standing there, his mouth slightly open. "What the hell was that?" he asked, his voice barely containing a laugh.

"You owe me," I said, trying to sound more confident than I felt. "That guy was seriously creeping me out. So... pretend you actually like me, okay?"

Adam's eyes danced with amusement, and he shook his head. "You seriously just kissed me in front of my friends and your sister, and now I owe you?"

I smirked. "Yes, and you'll thank me later. Trust me, that guy won't bother me again."

He stepped closer, leaning in as though to make sure no one else could hear. "So, what, you want me to play along for the rest of the night?"

I shrugged, trying to act casual, though my heart was still pounding from the adrenaline. "Why not? At least you won't have to pretend to be a saint."

Adam laughed, that familiar, easy chuckle that always seemed to get under my skin. "Fine. But just so you know, I'm going to make this *very* entertaining for my friends."

I shot him a mock glare, already regretting my impromptu plan. "Yeah, well, don't get too carried away."

As we walked back to the table, Sarah was practically bouncing in her seat. "Oh my god, I didn't know you had it in you, Rachel. That was *amazing*."

I shot her a half-smile, glancing at Adam. "Yeah, well, sometimes you've gotta take matters into your own hands."

As we settled into our seats, I couldn't quite shake the feeling that this summer was already shaping up to be far more complicated than I'd ever expected. But, as usual, Adam Harrison was at the center of it all.

Fourteen years ago

I stood with my arms crossed, glaring at Adam as he swung high on the rope swing hanging from the big oak tree. He was showing off—swinging so high I was sure he'd go flying into the lake.

"You're gonna break your neck one of these days, Adam!" I shouted, frustrated that he had to be such a showoff.

He didn't even flinch. Instead, he released the rope at the peak of his swing, launching himself into the air. My stomach dropped as I watched him land in a roll and pop back up like it was nothing.

"Don't be such a baby, Turner. You're just jealous you can't do it," he called out, brushing dirt off his jeans and grinning that smug, infuriating grin that always made me want to smack him.

"I'm not jealous!" I snapped, though it wasn't entirely true. Sure, part of me envied how carefree and fearless he was. But I'd never admit that to him. "You're just dumb. You're gonna hurt yourself one day, and then we'll see who's laughing."

Adam smirked, clearly not caring that I was mad. He stepped toward the swing, clearly planning to do it again, and I could feel the heat rising in my cheeks. Why did he always have to be so cocky?

He swung back onto the rope, kicking his legs out in front of him. The wind carried dust straight into my face as he laughed.

"Ugh!" I coughed, swiping at my eyes. "You're so gross, Adam."

"Am I?" he said, his voice oozing with mock innocence. He swung higher, giving me that look—the one that meant he knew exactly how to push my buttons. "Come on, Rachel. You used to love playing with me when we were little. Don't be such a grouch now."

I turned away, refusing to give him the satisfaction of a response. But it was so hard not to react to him—he always knew how to get under my skin. Always knew just what to say to make me lose my cool.

"Stop being such an idiot," I muttered, hoping he wouldn't hear, but of course, he did. He always did.

"I'm an idiot?" he called back, still swinging. "You used to think I was awesome. You sure about that now?"

He was grinning like an idiot himself, clearly enjoying how much he was getting to me. I clenched my fists, trying not to let him see how much his teasing was getting to me. Why did he have this effect on me? Why couldn't I just ignore him like everyone else?

I turned to walk toward the porch, not wanting to deal with him anymore. "I don't care," I muttered to myself.

"See you later, princess!" he yelled after me, but I didn't even respond, just marched inside, slamming the door behind me.

I leaned against the kitchen counter, breathing heavily, my heart pounding in a way that made no sense. I hated how easily he could make me feel like this—infuriated, embarrassed, but somehow still... curious. Why did I even care? Why did it bother me so much that Adam could make me lose my composure so easily?

The sound of his voice came through the window again.

"Hey, Turner! Bet I can jump higher than you can climb a tree!"

"Shut up, Adam!" I shouted back, storming out of the house, feeling an ache in my chest that I couldn't explain. The last thing I wanted to do was prove him right. But deep down, I knew it wouldn't stop me from trying to one-up him, just like I always had.

2

Adam

The whole bar was buzzing with energy, but I couldn't shake the feeling that tonight was different. Maybe it was because Rachel had just kissed me—*really* kissed me—in front of everyone. Or maybe it was because, after six years of teasing and keeping my distance, things suddenly felt a little... more real.

I leaned back against the bar, arms crossed, watching Rachel as she rejoined her sister and Kyle. She was trying to act like she hadn't just turned my world upside down with that kiss. And trust me, it had turned my world upside down. Her lips had been soft, urgent, as though she was determined to prove something. But for the life of me, I couldn't figure out if she'd kissed me to get rid of the creepy guy or because she *wanted* to kiss me.

Either way, it had felt damn good.

"You know," I said to my friends, trying to shake off the aftertaste of the kiss and keep my tone light, "this is going to be *so* much fun."

My friends, Dan and Luke, were watching me closely, and I could see the smirks forming. They knew something was up. Hell, I could barely keep a straight face myself. The whole "dating Rachel" act was a lot easier when I wasn't thinking about how *good* it had felt to have her in my arms for that split second.

"She seems like she's really into you," Luke said, raising an eyebrow. "That kiss didn't look like an act."

I chuckled, shaking my head. "Oh, trust me, it's definitely an act. Rachel and I have a long, storied history of being on opposite sides of the universe. She's just trying to get rid of some guy who was hitting on her."

Dan laughed. "I don't know, man. That looked pretty real to me."

I took a swig of my beer, trying to act like I wasn't affected by the way Rachel had kissed me in front of everyone. "She's a great actress, I'll give her that. Besides, I'm not one to kiss and tell." I tossed them a wink, knowing they'd pick up on the sarcasm.

But as I glanced back at Rachel, I saw her laugh with her sister, her eyes catching the light from the jukebox, and something inside me twisted. She was so damn beautiful when she wasn't looking at me with that fire in her eyes—when she wasn't shooting me down or making sarcastic remarks. There was a softness about her when she was with her family, and something about it drew me in like a magnet.

"Hey, man," Dan said, tapping me on the shoulder and breaking my thoughts. "You gonna stand there all night or go join the girl? Seems like you two are a bit of a spectacle tonight."

I blinked and shot him a look. "What do you mean by that?"

Luke laughed. "The whole bar's watching you two. Maybe you should play it up a little. They're dying to know if it's the real deal."

I hated the way my heart skipped at the thought of people seeing us that way. Rachel Turner, *my* girlfriend? It felt like the ultimate joke. But the more I thought about it, the more I couldn't ignore the feeling gnawing at me. I liked having her close. I liked the way my pulse raced when she kissed me.

"Fine," I muttered, feeling a little too eager to play along. "I'll go play my part."

I pushed off the bar and made my way over to their table, feeling the weight of every eye on me. Rachel was already glancing up at me, her face schooled into an expression I could barely read. She was sitting across from Sarah and Kyle, her lips pressed together in a line, but her eyes... her eyes flickered with something that made my stomach tighten.

"Is this where I'm supposed to make a grand entrance?" I asked with a grin, leaning against the table, putting on my most charming, carefree act.

Rachel raised an eyebrow. "Grand entrance? You mean, like you always do? You've perfected it."

"Gotta keep it interesting, right?" I teased, knowing she hated how effortlessly I could slide into the role of 'local legend' around here.

"Sure," she said dryly, but there was an edge to her voice I liked. "Just don't overdo it. We're supposed to be pretending."

I leaned in closer, lowering my voice just enough for only her to hear. "Oh, don't worry. I'll be very convincing. I promise."

Her eyes flickered toward mine for half a second, and there it was again—the faintest trace of something I couldn't name. Something I'd seen before, but never paid attention to. A challenge, maybe. Or maybe she was just trying to get a rise out of me.

"Good," she said, her voice just as low, her lips curling into a smile that was almost too perfect. "Because I really don't need you messing this up."

I held her gaze a little longer than necessary, the playful back-and-forth giving way to something else, something I wasn't ready to name.

The moment passed as quickly as it came, and Rachel shifted in her seat, suddenly all business again. "So, are we going to actually talk like a couple? Or is this just some kind of silent agreement to share drinks and dirty looks?"

I couldn't help but smirk. "I don't know about the dirty looks, but I'm game for whatever. We're 'dating,' right? Shouldn't be that hard."

She rolled her eyes, but there was something softening in her gaze. "I'll hold you to that, Adam. Just remember—you asked for this."

Yeah, I'd asked for it. But somewhere deep down, I knew I'd gotten more than I bargained for.

* * *

The morning air was crisp as I drove into work, the familiar winding roads of Lake Tahoe barely changing in the years I'd been away. I'd gotten used to the isolation of the place, the quiet mornings before the hustle of tourists and locals began filling the streets. But today, the silence in the car felt like it was pressing in on me.

I kept replaying last night in my head—the kiss. The way Rachel's lips had tasted, like a mix of surprise and defiance, like she wasn't sure why she'd kissed me but couldn't stop herself from doing it. I had a million questions swirling in my mind. Why did she do it? Did it mean anything? Did she feel the same rush I did?

I pushed the thought aside, focusing on the road as I pulled into the parking lot of the outdoor adventure company I worked for. The place was my sanctuary—a simple job, nothing fancy, but it kept me busy. Today was going to be just like any other day, right?

But the second I stepped out of my truck and felt the cool breeze hit my face, I found my mind drifting back to her. Rachel.

I'd seen her in that bar last night, sitting at the table with Sarah and Kyle, looking just a little out of place but still effortlessly stunning. There was something about the way she held herself, something that made her different from everyone else in town. Maybe it was the years away from Lake Tahoe, or maybe it was just that damn kiss—I couldn't put my finger on it, but I couldn't shake the way she'd looked at me, or how it had felt to kiss her in front of everyone.

Shaking my head, I headed inside, trying to force the thoughts away. I had a job to do. I'd been looking forward to a quiet day with some trail work and maybe helping a few of the newbies with their gear. But I couldn't focus. Not with her face in my head.

"Hey, Adam!" My coworker, Jake, waved me over as I entered the building, looking like he'd been up for hours already, a grin plastered across his face. "Glad you made it. You ready to hit the trail?"

"Yeah, sure," I muttered, trying to focus. "What are we doing today?"

Jake shot me a confused look, clearly picking up on the distracted vibe I was giving off. "You okay? You're kinda quiet today."

I gave him a half smile. "Yeah, just a lot on my mind. Got some stuff I need to work through."

Jake raised an eyebrow. "That's not like you. You've been Mr. Talkative and Ready for Anything since the season started."

"Just had a weird night, that's all," I said, trying to sound casual as I grabbed my gear. The last thing I wanted to do was dive into my personal life with Jake. Especially not when my personal life was full of complicated feelings about a woman who, for all intents and purposes, was still my childhood enemy.

Jake nodded, but I could see the concern in his eyes. "Well, if you need to talk, you know where to find me. Let's go get some work done, yeah?"

I didn't respond, just gave him a quick nod and followed him outside to the trucks. The whole time, I was trying to get my mind off Rachel, but it wasn't working. Every time I closed my eyes, I saw her: the way she'd looked at me when we'd made the "dating" thing official in front of the bar. Her lips on mine, the way my body had reacted. There was no denying it—I couldn't stop thinking about her.

And that drove me crazy.

We loaded up the truck with equipment and headed out to the trailhead. The whole time, I couldn't stop my mind from wandering back to Rachel. It was like she was daring me to see her in a way I hadn't before.

"I'll be back by 5," I told Jake as we finished setting up. "I'm gonna work on this section myself."

Jake gave me a strange look but didn't say anything, leaving me to the task. As I began checking the gear, tightening the straps on the bikes and making sure everything was in order, I found myself distracted again —it was like a loop I couldn't break free from.

Why the hell was I letting this get to me? I didn't have time to be thinking about Rachel Turner of all people. We were just playing a part. It was just a temporary situation.

But even as I tried to remind myself of that, something told me it wasn't going to be that simple.

I could almost hear her voice in my head, teasing me, challenging me to admit that maybe I was enjoying this. Maybe I wasn't just playing a part. But I wasn't ready to go there. Not yet.

The rest of the afternoon dragged on, and I tried my hardest to stay focused, but every minute felt like a battle between my thoughts of Rachel and my attempts to keep my cool. By the time I headed back to the cabin after work, the last vestiges of the sunset were fading, and I could feel that pull again.

I didn't know what was happening between us, but I knew I didn't want to stop it.

The only problem? I didn't know if I was ready to face the consequences of wanting her.

* * *

The house was quieter than usual when I picked up the phone. I hadn't talked to my family in a while, and I knew they'd start asking questions soon. I had already been avoiding calls for a couple of weeks, but today, I couldn't put it off any longer.

"Hey, Mom," I said, the words feeling a little heavier than they should. I hadn't expected the conversation to be so... uncomfortable. "How's it going?"

"Oh, Adam, it's good to hear your voice! We've been meaning to call you. How's work? Still keeping busy up there in Tahoe?"

"Yeah, always," I replied quickly, running a hand through my hair. "Just got back from a hike this morning. You know, the usual."

"Good, good. Keeping that adventure spirit alive, I see," she said with a soft chuckle. "I'm glad you're staying busy. And how's everything else? Anything new? Still living the solo life?"

I paused at her question, a lump forming in my throat. I could already hear the unspoken judgment in her voice, the way she always subtly implied that I should be doing more with my life than just focusing on work and the lake. The truth was, she had been asking about my love life for years, and every time, I had brushed her off. I was too busy, I'd tell her. It wasn't the right time. The truth was, I had never really been in any relationship long enough to bring anyone home. But recently, it felt like the pressure was building.

"Well, you know," I said, trying to sound casual. "I'm not really dating anyone right now. Just, you know, focused on work."

There was a pause on the other end, and I could almost hear her narrowing her eyes as if she was trying to decipher whether I was telling the truth or dodging the question again.

"Adam, sweetheart," she said, a little too sweetly. "You're twenty-seven now. You've been up there in Tahoe for years. You *really* should bring someone home to meet us sometime."

I winced at her words. Great, here we go again. My mom's version of "someone" was always the picture-perfect girlfriend, the kind of person she could show off to her friends. The kind of person I hadn't found yet—or, more honestly, the kind of person I wasn't ready to introduce to my family.

"Yeah, yeah, I know," I muttered, avoiding the real issue. "I've just been busy, you know? Haven't met anyone—"

"Well," she interrupted, "you know the Fourth of July's coming up. Your dad and I are throwing a little party, and we were hoping you could come down and join us. It's been ages since we've seen you, Adam. And you know, it would be so lovely to have you bring a guest along—someone special."

The words hit me like a ton of bricks. *Someone special.* I ran a hand through my hair again, my mind suddenly racing. The last thing I wanted was to be put on the spot like this. The thought of introducing anyone to my family, especially someone I was *pretending* to date, made my stomach turn. But there was no backing out now. My mom was relentless when it came to this stuff.

I was silent for a moment, trying to think of something that would make this conversation end without making a fool of myself. But the words came out before I could stop them.

"Uh... actually," I said, the words spilling out too quickly, "I do have someone... I've been seeing someone. Rachel. Rachel Turner."

The silence on the other end was deafening. I could practically hear my mom's brain working as she processed the information.

"Rachel Turner?" she repeated, sounding surprised, and maybe a little too interested. "As in, *the* Rachel Turner?"

I groaned inwardly. "Yeah, *that* Rachel Turner. You remember her, right? We were neighbors when we were kids."

"Oh, of course!" my mom exclaimed, clearly remembering. "She was always such a sweet girl! Well, Adam, that's wonderful! Why didn't you tell us sooner? We'd love to meet her! You must bring her to the party. We'll make sure everything is perfect."

I blinked in surprise. My mom never wasted time when it came to matchmaking. Rachel and I had just started pretending to date, and here I was, agreeing to take her to a family party. But what else could I say? My mom was already planning on meeting Rachel, whether I liked it or not.

"Yeah, okay. I'll... I'll let her know," I said, my voice sounding hoarse even to my own ears.

"That's my boy," my mom said with a satisfied sigh. "I'm so glad to hear you've found someone! We'll have a great time, I'm sure of it. I'll make sure we have enough food and drinks—can't wait to see you both! Oh, and don't worry about the details. Just make sure she knows how much we're looking forward to seeing her again after all these years."

"Yeah, Mom, I'll let her know," I said, not really knowing what I was getting myself into.

"Great! I'll talk to you soon, sweetheart. We'll be expecting you both on the Fourth!"

I hung up the phone, feeling a mix of dread and disbelief. Rachel was going to *love* this.

What the hell had I just gotten myself into?

Eight years ago

I watched Rachel from across the yard, her focus entirely on the book she was reading, sitting on the edge of the old porch swing. She was always so serious, so intent on whatever she did—always with that furrow in her brow like she was solving the world's problems with every page she turned. It made me want to mess with her.

I didn't even know why I did it, really. There was just something about her that got under my skin. Something about how she always acted like she had it all together, like she didn't care about anything. I used to think it was annoying, but lately, I was starting to see it differently. I'd catch myself looking at her more than I probably should. But that didn't mean I was going to go all soft on her. No way. Rachel Turner would never get the satisfaction of knowing she had any effect on me.

Still, I couldn't resist.

I grabbed the football from where I'd left it by the tree, walked over to her spot on the porch, and tossed it lightly in the air. "Hey, bookworm. Do you know the difference between a touchdown and an interception?"

She didn't even look up from her book. "Go away, Adam."

Her voice was quiet, but firm—so typical. But it didn't stop me. It never did.

"You sure? You look like you could use a little excitement in your life." I stepped closer, dropping the ball on the ground in front of her and kicking it gently with my foot toward her. "Maybe I could teach you something about the game. You know, if you ever wanted to learn."

She sighed dramatically, finally lowering her book and giving me that look—the one that said she was one comment away from losing her patience with me. "I don't need you to teach me anything. I'm fine," she said, rolling her eyes.

But the way she bit the edge of her lip told me something different. I could tell she was holding back a smile, which made my chest tighten in a way I couldn't explain. I was so used to getting under her skin, but this time, it felt... different.

"Fine, if you don't want to learn, I guess I'll just have to throw a touchdown all by myself." I smiled, taking a few steps back, pretending like I was about to launch the ball down the yard.

She narrowed her eyes. "You're so dramatic. Just go away already."

But I wasn't done. There was no way I could leave now. "You sure? You know, you could come watch me score. Might be good for your... education," I teased, making it sound like I was being cocky. The words just came out of my mouth, but what I really wanted to say was, I just want you to notice me, Rachel. I want you to look at me the way you look at everything else.

She glared at me, clearly deciding to ignore me, but I could see her shoulders stiffen. I loved the way I could get to her, even when I wasn't trying.

"I don't need your attention," she muttered under her breath, though I caught the faintest blush creeping up her neck.

I shoved my hands into my pockets, trying to play it off like I wasn't affected by that. It was just Rachel being Rachel. But that little blush, that soft hint of embarrassment—it did something to me. Made me wonder why I couldn't shake the feeling that maybe, just maybe, she didn't completely hate me. Maybe I was wrong. Maybe, when I was being an idiot, she was actually paying attention to me.

"Suit yourself," I said, grinning as I turned back toward the yard and tossed the ball in the air again, pretending not to notice that she was watching me. I didn't want to admit it, but I kind of liked how she noticed me. I liked that she cared enough to call me out on my nonsense. Even though she'd never say it, I could tell she liked when I pushed her buttons.

I tossed the ball up higher, just for the thrill of it. But when it sailed back down toward me, I didn't catch it as easily as I usually would. I missed, and it bounced right off the ground and rolled toward her.

I had no choice but to jog over to retrieve it.

Rachel was already standing up, holding out the ball toward me.

"Need help?" she asked, her voice softer than usual.

I shrugged, pretending like it didn't bother me. "Nah, I've got it," I said, but as I reached for the ball, our hands brushed against each other. I felt a weird spark—a jolt of heat that shot up my arm. My heart skipped a beat, and I could've sworn I saw the same flush on her cheeks that I had noticed before.

I pulled my hand back, trying to act like nothing had happened.

But deep down, I knew one thing for sure: I wanted Rachel Turner to notice me. I just couldn't admit it. Not yet. Not when I was so damn good at pretending I didn't care.

3

Rachel

I was sitting at the kitchen table, sipping a cup of coffee, when my phone buzzed in my pocket. I pulled it out to see a message from Adam.

Hey, got something to tell you. Can we talk?

I frowned at the screen. What now? After the bar last night, I figured we were on the same page about this whole "pretending to date" thing, but now I wasn't so sure. I hesitated for a moment, then typed back.

Sure. What's up?

A few minutes later, my phone buzzed again.

My mom is hosting a Fourth of July party, and she's already asked me to bring someone... guess who that someone is?

I blinked, then groaned aloud. Of course his mom would want to meet me. This wasn't just a fake relationship anymore; it was real enough to involve family. And not just any family—his family.

You're kidding. She's already inviting me?

I could almost hear his sigh through the text.

Not quite. But I told her I was seeing someone. So now she wants to meet you.

I stared at the message for a moment, trying to process the absurdity of it all. My mind raced with what this would mean—being thrown into Adam's world like that, being around his family, pretending to be someone I wasn't, all for the sake of keeping up the illusion.

I ran a hand through my hair, trying to think of how to respond. I didn't want to back out. The idea of not going would just lead to more questions from my own family, especially since my sister had already been grilling me about my love life. And honestly, I hadn't had a good reason to talk to them about it—until now.

I quickly typed back.

Fine. But we need a plan. I'm not just going to show up and pretend everything's fine without something to back it up. And I need something to get my family off my back, too. This is the perfect opportunity to kill two birds with one stone.

A few seconds later, Adam's reply came through.

*Yeah, I figured you'd want a plan. How about we agree to do a couple of dates before the party so it seems like we've actually been seeing each other for a while? I'll be honest with you, my mom is *really* excited about this, and she'll want to know all the details.*

I bit my lip, my mind already racing with potential options. The idea of spending more time with Adam was... complicated. But it would work. It had to. For both of us.

Okay, but we need to make it believable. Like, we've been seeing each other for weeks, not just one night. Let's do a few things that will look like we've been dating for a while.

I paused before adding, *We can even pretend to get to know each other better over the next couple of weeks. That way it'll seem natural when we show up to your family's party.*

I could almost feel Adam's smirk through the phone as his reply came through quickly.

That's exactly what I was thinking. We can go on a couple of dinners, do some things in town—whatever we need to sell this. No one will question it if we make it look like we've been together for a bit.

I leaned back in my chair, taking a deep breath. This was insane. But I had no other choice if I wanted to avoid more awkward conversations with my family. And, truth be told, Adam was right. This would get my parents off my back, at least for a while.

Alright. But no funny business, okay? We stick to the plan, and nothing gets weird. This is just for our families, nothing else.

I watched the dots appear and disappear as he typed his response. When it finally came, I half-expected him to be sarcastic, to make some offhand comment about how much *fun* this would be. But instead, his reply was short and to the point.

Agreed. I'll call you later to figure out the details.

Good. And Adam?

Yeah?

You owe me for this.

He responded quickly with a string of laughing emojis, but I could tell he wasn't kidding.

I know. I'm buying dinner next time. Promise.

I smirked, leaning back against the chair and letting out a breath I hadn't realized I'd been holding. This was happening. We were going to do this—pretend to date for the sake of our families. And in the process, we'd probably end up spending way too much time together. Maybe more than either of us had bargained for. But that was the deal we'd struck, and for now, it was the only way out.

* * *

The phone rang twice before my mom picked up. I took a deep breath and steeled myself for what was about to come. I hadn't even told her I was back in Tahoe yet, let alone about my new situation with Adam. But with the Fourth of July coming up in just a few weeks and everyone asking what my plans were, I had no choice but to spill the beans.

"Hey, Mom," I said, trying to sound casual, even though my heart was pounding. "How's everything?"

"Rachel! Oh my gosh, I was just about to call you. We've been meaning to check in. How's Tahoe? Is it beautiful up there?"

"Yeah, it's great," I said, glancing out the window at the glistening lake. "Really nice. Just getting back into the swing of things."

"Good, good," she replied, sounding pleased. "So what are your plans for the Fourth of July? You must be heading out to the big party, right?"

I winced. The big party she was talking about was the one at my aunt's house—the usual family gathering. I knew she was expecting me to be there, probably with someone, just like last year when I'd had to explain why I didn't have a "serious boyfriend" like she thought I should. But now I was stuck in the middle of this whole fake relationship with Adam, and I needed to come up with something that sounded convincing.

I hesitated for a moment, looking around the room, wondering if there was a way to smooth this over without making it awkward.

"Well, actually," I said, drawing the words out slowly, "I've been seeing someone. His name's Adam. Adam Harrison."

There was a pause on the other end of the line, and I could practically hear her brain working. My mom was great at reading between the lines, and I could tell she wasn't buying the casual tone I was trying to put on. But, to her credit, she didn't press me for details right away.

"Adam Harrison?" she repeated, a little too intrigued. "I think I remember him. Didn't he live next door when you were a kid?"

"Yeah," I replied, shifting uncomfortably. "We were neighbors growing up. We've been in touch again recently."

"Interesting," my mom said, sounding like she was making mental notes. "So, you're seeing him now?"

I quickly pushed forward, trying to ease her into this. "Yeah. We've been... hanging out, you know? It's been good. We're actually going to the Fourth of July party together. We have to go to his family's party later in the evening, but we'll make it work."

There was a noticeable shift in her tone, and I could hear her sitting up straighter. "Really? That's wonderful, Rachel! I'm so glad you've finally found someone. And it's Adam, of all people. Well, that makes it even better! I think that'll be so fun for everyone to see. Your dad will be thrilled."

I couldn't help the small sigh of relief that escaped my lips. She was buying it—mostly.

"I'm glad you're happy about it," I said, trying to keep the conversation light. "I'll introduce you to him at the party, of course. He's looking forward to meeting everyone."

"That's fantastic! We'll have to make sure there's plenty of food, drinks, and of course, you two will have the best spot at the barbecue. Oh, and don't forget to tell Adam we're expecting him to be there early. Your father and I like to have the place set up well before the crowds start showing up."

"Of course, Mom. We'll be there," I said, mentally crossing my fingers that Adam wouldn't somehow back out last minute. He probably wouldn't, but I knew it would be awkward for both of us if things got any more real than they already were.

"Well, it sounds like you've got a solid plan for the Fourth. I'm so excited to meet Adam. And Rachel, honey, I know I've been on you about this before, but I'm really happy for you. You've always been so focused on your career, but I think having someone to share it with will make everything even better."

"Thanks, Mom," I said, not sure what else to say. "I'll keep you updated, and I'll let you know if anything changes."

"You know we're here for you, right? We just want the best for you."

"I know, Mom," I replied, trying to keep my tone light. "I'll see you at the party."

"Can't wait! I'm so glad you're bringing him. It's going to be a wonderful weekend!"

We hung up, and I sat there for a moment, staring at my phone. The conversation had gone surprisingly well. My mom seemed thrilled about Adam, even if I could tell she was dying to know all the details. But I had no intention of giving them all away just yet.

I knew what I was getting myself into. This was all temporary. Just a couple of weeks of pretending to be something I wasn't. No big deal. Right?

* * *

I found Sarah sitting on the couch, scrolling through her phone, looking way too comfortable. Her eyes flicked up when I walked in, and the second she saw me, she grinned like she'd just uncovered some juicy gossip.

"So," she began, the corner of her mouth curling up into a teasing smile, "how's the 'relationship' with Adam going?"

I sighed dramatically and dropped into the armchair across from her. "Oh, don't act like you don't already know,"

I muttered. "I'm not in the mood for you to play detective, Sarah."

She let out a small laugh, tossing her phone onto the coffee table. "Well, I *was* there when you kissed him last night," she said, her eyes sparkling with amusement. "But I'm dying to hear the rest of the story. So, how's it going? Still pretending to date?"

I groaned and flopped back against the chair, rubbing my temples. "Ugh, don't remind me. I just called Mom, and she's already planning the entire Fourth of July around us. I can't even breathe without her bringing up Adam like she's already in love with him."

Sarah raised an eyebrow, clearly enjoying my frustration. "That's because she thinks you've finally found someone. I mean, you two did kiss in front of a bar full of people, so... kinda hard to argue with that."

I shot her a glare. "I didn't kiss him because I wanted to, Sarah. It was to get that creepy guy off my back! I didn't exactly plan on having my entire family think I'm really with Adam."

Sarah snickered. "Yeah, right. So, now you're stuck pretending to date him for real. What's your plan for this whole thing? Just keep playing the part?"

"Pretty much," I said with a resigned sigh. "It's not like I have a choice. My mom is practically counting down the days to meet him, and now Adam's family is expecting me to show up at their Fourth of July party. You should've heard my mom—it's like I'm the first person in history to actually date someone."

Sarah looked at me with mock sympathy. "Well, it's about time. But hey, I can't blame you for going along with it. Free ride to not get interrogated about your non-existent love life? Sounds like a win."

I narrowed my eyes at her. "I'm really not sure I'm ready to spend the whole summer pretending, though. You know I can't lie to my mom for long. And Adam's definitely not the kind of guy I'd actually date."

She snorted, clearly amused. "Yeah, because we all know you'd rather be alone forever than be caught kissing him again."

"Shut up," I said, but my cheeks flushed anyway. It wasn't that simple. I didn't *want* to kiss him again. But that kiss last night had been... confusing. It wasn't as bad as I thought it would be, and that scared me more than I cared to admit.

"So, when do I get to meet this 'boyfriend' of yours?" she asked, leaning forward, clearly amused by the idea of me actually introducing Adam as my fake boyfriend.

"He's coming to the Fourth of July party," I said, trying to sound casual about it. "And don't get any ideas. I'm trusting you to keep this whole thing under wraps. I don't need anyone else getting in on the joke."

"Oh, you can count on me," Sarah said, raising her hand like she was swearing an oath. "I'll keep it secret. But I do expect a full report after you two pull this off, because I'm sure it's going to be hilarious."

I rolled my eyes but couldn't help the small laugh that slipped out. "You're the worst. You know that, right?"

She grinned. "Hey, someone's got to have fun with this. And don't worry. I won't tell anyone. But I do want to know what happens when you start pretending for real. That's going to be interesting."

"Please don't," I groaned. "If you say anything, I swear I'll—"

"Relax," she said, cutting me off. "I won't ruin your little charade. But you've got to admit, this is a great story. You and Adam, the fake couple, playing it cool in front of your family. I can already see the awkwardness unfolding."

I shot her a warning look, but a part of me couldn't help but laugh. "This is seriously going to be the worst summer of my life."

"Oh, I don't know. I think it's going to be the best," she teased. "And I'm going to make sure I'm in the front row when you and Adam try to make this work. I'm going to have popcorn ready."

4

Rachel

The bells over the door jingled as we walked into Sweet Scoops, Tahoe's famous little ice cream shop. The air inside was heavy with the smell of fresh waffle cones and melted chocolate, and it instantly took me back to summers as a kid, licking sticky fingers after devouring massive scoops of mint chocolate chip.

Adam followed me inside, hands in his pockets as he looked around with that easygoing smirk that always seemed to be plastered on his face lately. I couldn't tell if he was amused by the whole situation or just by watching me squirm. Probably both.

"So, this is what you call a date?" he teased, eyeing the chalkboard menu filled with flavors like 'Campfire Marshmallow' and 'Tahoe Pine Nut.'

I rolled my eyes and ignored his smug tone. "You agreed to it, didn't you? Besides, everyone loves ice cream."

He raised an eyebrow. "True. But I just wasn't expecting something so... romantic."

I smirked back at him. "Please. You don't deserve anything fancier."

He laughed, stepping up to the counter. "Alright, I'll bite. What's your flavor?"

The woman behind the counter looked expectantly at me, and I scanned the options, torn between sticking to my childhood favorite or trying something new.

"I'll have a scoop of mint chocolate chip," I decided finally, giving in to nostalgia. "In a waffle cone, please."

Adam nodded approvingly. "A classic. Guess I'll keep it simple, too. One scoop of rocky road, also in a waffle cone."

As we waited for our cones, Adam leaned casually against the counter and gave me an exaggerated look. "So, Rachel, what made you want to go out with a guy like me?"

I snorted, unable to stop myself from playing along. "Oh, you know, I just couldn't resist the charm of my childhood enemy," I shot back. "I mean, what's not to love about someone who used to hide my stuff and make my life miserable?"

He grinned, not missing a beat. "So you admit you liked the attention?"

I narrowed my eyes, though the hint of a smile was already tugging at the corners of my lips. "In your dreams, Harrison."

He laughed, taking his cone when the woman handed it over, then waited for me to get mine. We found a small table near the window, the bright sunshine streaming in, casting golden rays over the tiny shop. Outside, people strolled along the lake's edge, enjoying the early summer warmth.

I took a lick of my ice cream, the familiar minty sweetness instantly bringing back memories. Adam watched me, amusement dancing in his eyes. "You know, if this was a real date, I'd think you were playing hard to get."

"Oh, please," I scoffed. "I'd say I'm just playing it safe. You're still the guy who stuck gum in my hair in seventh grade."

He winced, looking genuinely sorry, though there was a hint of a smile lurking behind his expression. "I was twelve! And, for the record, that was an accident."

I raised an eyebrow. "Yeah, sure. Total accident that the gum happened to land in my hair when you threw it across the room?"

He looked down at his cone, hiding a laugh. "Alright, maybe it was slightly intentional. But I'm a changed man now. No gum, I promise."

We both laughed, the banter feeling oddly comfortable—like falling back into an old rhythm. Despite everything, I had to admit it was... nice, sitting here with him, laughing about the past.

"So," he said, leaning forward slightly, "since this is our *first date,* maybe you should tell me something real. You know, pretend we're actually trying to get to know each other."

"Oh, you think I don't already know everything about you?"

He shook his head. "I'm serious. Tell me something I don't know."

I thought for a moment, taking another lick of my ice cream. "Alright. When I was ten, I actually tried running away. Packed a bag, snuck out in the middle of the night, made it all the way down the block before I realized I'd forgotten to pack snacks. I came back because I got hungry."

He chuckled, shaking his head. "Wow, the brave Rachel Turner, foiled by hunger. I would've thought you'd make it farther."

I rolled my eyes. "Shows what you know. I was a serious kid, alright?"

"Yeah, yeah, I can see that," he said, nodding. "A rebel at heart."

"Exactly," I said, grinning despite myself.

He was quiet for a moment, the playful teasing giving way to something more sincere. "It's good to see you like this, Turner. I mean... laughing and all. Maybe this fake dating thing isn't so bad after all."

I glanced away, a strange warmth settling in my chest. This was supposed to be pretend, and here we were, sitting across from each other, sharing memories like old friends. And as much as I wanted to brush it off as just an act, something about the way he looked at me made it feel a little too real.

Clearing my throat, I forced a smile and held up my cone. "To fake dates," I said, trying to keep the mood light.

He smiled, clinking his cone against mine. "To fake dates."

* * *

The drive back from Sweet Scoops was filled with laughter and lighthearted teasing, but by the time we pulled up to my family's cabin, the quiet evening was setting in, with the sun casting a warm, golden glow over the lake.

Adam hopped out of the car, stretching as he looked around the yard. "So, what's next? Or do you just plan to kick me out now that the ice cream has done its job?"

I raised an eyebrow, smirking. "Not yet. I still need you to help me get through the Fourth of July. I can't have you abandoning ship just because we had a decent time on one fake date."

He chuckled, shrugging. "Fair point. So, what do you usually do around here? I can't imagine a summer in Tahoe is complete without some sort of outdoor activity."

I thought for a moment, glancing around the yard. My gaze landed on the stack of lawn games tucked under the porch. "Well, since you're here... how are you at cornhole?"

His face lit up with a competitive grin. "You're on. But only if you're ready to lose."

"Oh, please," I said, already heading to grab the game set. "I don't lose at cornhole."

He helped me set up the boards and tossed me a red bean bag. I took my spot on the lawn, feeling a mix of excitement and nerves. It was weird, being with Adam like this. It didn't feel forced or awkward. Instead, there was this odd sense of familiarity, like we'd done this a hundred times before.

"Ladies first," he said, smirking as he stepped back to give me room.

"Thank you, kind sir," I replied with a mock curtsy, lining up my shot.

With a flick of my wrist, I tossed the bean bag, watching as it hit the board and slid neatly into the hole. I couldn't help but flash a smug grin. "See? Not a chance you're winning this."

Adam raised his eyebrows, impressed. "Alright, okay. One point for you. But don't get cocky."

He tossed his own bean bag, and, of course, it also went straight in. I rolled my eyes. "Alright, so you're not bad at this. Beginner's luck."

"Oh, is that what it is?" he asked, grinning as he went to retrieve the bags.

We settled into a rhythm, taking turns tossing the bags, each one-upping the other. The game quickly turned into a battle of wits and competitive banter.

"Okay, if I win this round, you owe me a rematch tomorrow," he said, narrowing his eyes in determination.

"If I win, you have to tell me something embarrassing from your childhood," I countered, tossing my bean bag with a grin.

His expression faltered for a split second. "Something embarrassing? That's dangerous territory."

"Consider it your penalty for losing," I teased, shrugging. "Shouldn't be a problem if you're as good as you think you are."

He rolled his eyes, laughing. "Fine. But you'd better be ready to lose, because there's nothing I'd rather avoid than sharing those stories."

With that, he tossed his bean bag—and, to my surprise, it missed the board entirely, skidding across the grass. I burst out laughing, clutching my sides as I watched his confident expression dissolve.

"Oh my god, I actually made you choke!" I laughed, pointing at the bean bag lying pitifully on the grass. "Adam Harrison, Tahoe's finest competitor, finally messed up."

"Don't get too excited," he grumbled, trying to look unbothered. But the faint blush creeping up his cheeks gave him away. "One bad throw doesn't mean anything."

"Oh, it means everything," I replied, picking up the last bean bag and tossing it effortlessly onto the board, securing my victory. "Looks like you owe me a story."

He groaned, running a hand through his hair. "Alright, alright. You win. But keep in mind, you asked for it."

I crossed my arms, waiting expectantly. "This better be good."

He rubbed the back of his neck, clearly reluctant. "Okay, when I was like... ten, I thought it would be a good idea to impress my friends by showing them I could make a 'mudslide' down a hill near my house. It had just rained, so I figured, why not? I took a running leap, slid halfway down... and face-planted in the mud right in front of everyone."

I couldn't help it—I burst out laughing. "Oh, that's amazing. Why have I never heard this story before?"

"Because I've kept it buried for a reason," he muttered, a grin breaking through despite his embarrassment.

The sun began to sink lower, casting a warm, orange glow over the yard. Somehow, standing here with Adam felt right, like a small slice of summer I hadn't expected to find. There was an ease between us now, a genuine warmth that was starting to blur the lines between what was real and what was pretend.

"So," he said, picking up the bean bags again, "how about that rematch?"

I took a deep breath, feeling the rush of excitement building all over again. "You're on, Harrison. Just be prepared to lose."

* * *

The rumble of Adam's truck pulling up outside was my only warning. I'd barely grabbed my bag and slipped on my shoes before he was honking, his typical grin already in place through the open window.

"Ready, Turner?" he called out as I hopped down the porch steps and made my way over.

"Ready as I'll ever be," I shot back, climbing into the passenger seat. The familiar scent of leather and pine filled the truck, and I tried not to let the fact that it felt weirdly nice being here get to me. This wasn't a real date; it was just one of many to keep up our cover.

"So, where are we off to today?" I asked, buckling up.

Adam put the truck in gear, glancing over at me with that mischievous glint in his eyes. "I thought we'd start with coffee. There's this little spot I know about. And no," he added with a smirk, "it's not Starbucks. I know you're probably judging my coffee shop choices already."

I gave him a mock look of offense. "Hey, I'm an iced coffee person, not a coffee snob. And if this place has anything close to caffeine, it'll be fine by me."

He chuckled as he pulled onto the main road, heading toward town. We fell into an easy silence, the kind that felt natural in a way I wasn't expecting. A few minutes later, we turned down a small side street and stopped in front of a tiny, log-cabin-style café with wooden benches outside and string lights twinkling from the porch beams.

"This is it?" I asked, raising an eyebrow as I took in the rustic little spot.

He looked almost proud, hopping out and coming around to open my door. "Yep, best coffee in Tahoe. Trust me."

I rolled my eyes but followed him inside, and as soon as the rich scent of coffee beans and baked goods hit me, I had to admit it was a good choice. Inside, the café had a cozy, eclectic vibe, with mismatched chairs, old photos on the walls, and plants hanging from every corner. A chalkboard behind the counter listed drinks and pastries in colorful, looping handwriting.

Adam ordered a black coffee—typical—and I got an iced caramel latte. As we waited, he glanced around the shop, hands tucked into his pockets, looking oddly at ease.

"So, why this place?" I asked, taking a sip of my drink once our order was ready. "I feel like you have a soft spot for little hidden spots like this."

He shrugged, walking us over to a small table near the window. "I don't know. It's been here forever. I used to come here after work when I first moved back to Tahoe. Just got attached, I guess."

I studied him for a moment, surprised by the admission. "I wouldn't have pegged you as the nostalgic type."

He looked up, giving a slight smirk. "Maybe I'm just full of surprises. But hey, what about you? You've spent most of your life here—what's your favorite spot in Tahoe?"

"Oh, that's easy," I replied, warming up to the conversation. "There's this overlook near the lake, up on one of the hiking trails. When the sun sets, the whole place lights up in pinks and purples. It's amazing."

Adam looked thoughtful, leaning back in his chair. "You'll have to show me sometime. I don't think I've ever been up there."

I shrugged, trying to keep it casual. "Maybe. If you can keep up."

He laughed, taking a sip of his coffee. "Is that a challenge?"

"Always," I said, a small smile tugging at my lips.

We sat there, talking over coffee for a while longer than I'd expected. I kept reminding myself this was just another staged moment, something to get us through the next "date" and convince everyone we were a real couple. But the more we talked, the more I realized how easy it was to just sit and laugh with him, like we'd done it a hundred times before.

After a while, Adam glanced at his watch. "Alright, you ready to get going?"

"Where are we going, exactly?" I asked, a little curious.

"Guess you'll just have to wait and see," he said, his eyes glinting with that familiar mischief. He stood up, reaching his hand out to help me out of my seat. It felt natural to take it, even as my heart did a tiny flip I was determined to ignore.

5

Rachel

The beach at Camp Richardson was bustling with people when we arrived, a mix of families, locals, and sunbathers lounging on towels or splashing in the lake. A rainbow of umbrellas littered the beach, and faint music played from the nearby restaurant. The air smelled like sunscreen and lake water, and a soft breeze was blowing across the sand, ruffling the tops of the tall pines. A mama and her baby ducks paddled lazily around the swimmers and seagulls flew overhead. The beach was a mix of sand and fine pebbles, and the water line was filled with larger rocks, leading out into the crisp cool water.

Adam tossed his towel over his shoulder, looking over at me with that easy grin that had become way too familiar. "Last chance to back out. Think you can keep up with me in the water, Turner?"

I rolled my eyes, adjusting my sunglasses as I laid out my towel. "What is it with you and thinking I can't keep up? News flash: I grew up here. The lake is practically my second home."

He snorted, kicking off his flip-flops and spreading out his own towel beside mine. "I'll believe it when I see it. Want to make it interesting?"

I narrowed my eyes, catching the hint of a challenge in his tone. "Like a bet?"

He shrugged, his smirk deepening. "Sure. If I win, you owe me a favor—whatever I want."

"And if I win?" I asked, crossing my arms.

His eyes glinted in the sun. "Then you get one free favor from me. Anything."

I pretended to consider, even though I was already mentally rehearsing my victory speech. "Fine. But don't say I didn't warn you."

Without waiting for a response, I pulled off my cover-up and started toward the lake, feeling the sand warming my feet as I made my way to the edge. I could hear him following close behind, his footsteps crunching softly in the sand.

The water was cool against my legs as I waded in, and when I turned around, Adam was right beside me, grinning like a kid about to do something stupid. Behind him, I could see the cabins that lined where the beach met the tree-line, accompanied by volleyball courts with players eager to win. The water was scattered with swimmers, but was less crowded by the edge of the swimming area, marked off by a rope attached to buoys. The water lapped against my skin as I treaded deeper into the waves.

"First one to the buoy?" he challenged, nodding toward a bright orange buoy a little ways out.

"You're on," I said, giving him a head start as I launched forward, kicking up water as I swam. He laughed, splashing water in my direction as he sped ahead, clearly enjoying the competition.

But I'd spent too many summers swimming here to let him beat me. I dug in, matching his pace, until I pulled ahead just enough to reach the buoy first, tapping it triumphantly.

I turned to see him stop just short of it, giving me a half-hearted glare. "Fine, I'll admit it. You're faster than you look."

I grinned, treading water beside him. "And you're slower than you talk. Guess that makes me the winner, huh?"

He splashed a handful of water at me, his expression playful. "Careful, Turner. You might make me think you're actually having fun."

I splashed him back, laughing as he pretended to be offended. "Who says I'm not?"

We hung there in the water for a moment, catching our breath, the sun glinting off the lake and casting shimmers across the waves. I was almost surprised at how easy it was to just... be here with him, laughing like we hadn't spent years at each other's throats.

"Alright," he said, nodding back toward shore. "Let's head in. I'm getting hungry, and I'm sure you want to cash in on that favor sooner rather than later."

As we swam back, he reached the shore just before I did, turning around to offer me a hand out of the water. I took it, feeling the warmth of his hand against mine as he helped me onto the sand.

"Impressive race," he said as we walked back to our towels. "But I wouldn't get too cocky. You're still the one who owes me a favor."

I rolled my eyes, plopping down onto my towel and leaning back to soak up the sun. "Dream on, Harrison. You're the one who agreed to the terms, remember?"

He sat down beside me, shaking his head in amusement. "I know. I just like to see how far I can push my luck."

We spent the next few hours swimming and lounging on the sand, talking about everything and nothing. We walked down the beach towards the dock that tourists and locals alike jumped off of. Adam challenged me to flips and dives into the deep water until we could no longer catch our breaths. Eventually, the afternoon heat got the best of us, and I found myself drifting into a light doze, the sun warming my skin as the lake waves lapped gently against the shore.

When I opened my eyes, Adam was leaning back on his elbows beside me, watching the water. His face was relaxed, and for once, there was no smirk, no teasing glint in his eye. Just an ease that made him look... different. Less like the guy who'd always known how to get under my skin and more like someone I might actually want to spend time with.

Feeling his gaze shift toward me, I quickly looked away, clearing my throat. "Alright," I said, sitting up. "What's next on this so-called date of ours?"

He grinned, the playful look back in full force. "Well, now that you mention it, there's this little food stand up the beach. Best fish tacos you'll ever have."

I shrugged, trying to act casual. "I could be persuaded to eat."

As we walked up the beach, side by side, I couldn't help but smile, a warmth spreading through me that had nothing to do with the sun. Whatever this fake relationship was turning into, I was starting to think I didn't mind so much after all.

The line at the taco stand was short, and as soon as we reached the window, I could smell the blend of spices, cilantro, and lime wafting through the air. Adam stepped up to order, glancing back at me.

"Two fish tacos?" he asked, raising an eyebrow with a small smile. "Or are you going to claim you can eat more than I can?"

I crossed my arms, smirking back. "I'll take three, actually. Just to prove a point."

He chuckled, shaking his head as he placed the order. "Alright, three fish tacos for the lady. And three for me. We'll see who finishes first."

We grabbed our tacos and found a spot at a small picnic table in the shade of a large pine tree, overlooking the lake. The water was glinting in the late afternoon sun, and I could hear the faint sounds of kids laughing and people chatting nearby. For a second, it felt like just another summer day, not a setup between two people faking a relationship.

I unwrapped my first taco, squeezing a bit of lime over the top and taking a bite. The flavors hit me immediately—the crunch of cabbage, the spice of the fish, and a hint of tangy salsa. "Oh my god, this is amazing," I said, practically melting into my seat.

Adam nodded, his mouth full as he took a big bite of his own. "Told you," he said, grinning. "Best fish tacos in Tahoe. And I know my tacos."

"Oh, so now you're a taco expert?" I teased, taking another bite. "I thought you were just a small-town boy who couldn't beat me at cornhole."

He smirked, leaning back and taking his time with the food. "I'm a man of many talents. Just because you haven't seen them all yet doesn't mean they aren't there."

I rolled my eyes, but I couldn't help the smile tugging at my lips. "So, what other hidden talents should I be watching out for, then? Maybe a magic trick?"

"Please," he said, smirking. "Magic's kid stuff. But I do make a mean s'more."

I laughed, leaning forward. "Oh, that's impressive. Almost as impressive as your taco knowledge. I'm really starting to wonder why you're still single."

He laughed too, but I saw something flicker in his eyes, something he quickly masked. "Maybe I just haven't found anyone who appreciates my talents. Or maybe... I don't know, maybe I was waiting for the right person to pretend-date me."

"Lucky me," I replied, feeling a warmth spread in my chest.

We ate in companionable silence for a while, with him glancing up every so often to throw in another light jab about my taco-eating technique or the way I'd squeeze just a little too much lime on each bite. But I didn't mind the teasing; in fact, it felt... nice. Like there was some kind of shared understanding between us, even if it was just for show.

After polishing off my third taco, I leaned back with a satisfied sigh, noticing he was already done with his.

"I guess that means you win," I admitted, giving him a mock-pout.

He shrugged, grinning as he gathered up the empty wrappers. "It was a close race. But don't worry, there's plenty more where that came from. You can challenge me again next time."

I scoffed. "Next time? Getting a little ahead of yourself, aren't you?"

He just shrugged, his smile easy. "Guess we'll see."

As we tossed our wrappers in the trash and started walking back toward the truck, I couldn't help but wonder when I'd started to look forward to these moments. Moments that felt too real for something we were both pretending at.

But for now, I pushed the thought aside, following him back to the truck, ready for whatever came next.

* * *

I let out a long sigh as I walked up the steps to the cabin and opened the door, the lingering scent of sunscreen and lake water clinging to my skin. The day at Camp Richardson had been fun—too fun, honestly. More fun than any "fake" date should be.

I was still thinking about the way Adam had looked at me over fish tacos when I heard Sarah call out from the living room. "Hey! How was your date?"

I groaned, half-smiling as I dropped my bag and wandered into the living room where she was sprawled out on the couch with a book. She glanced up, a playful glint in her eye as she took in my slightly sunburned cheeks.

"It was... fine," I said, trying to sound casual as I grabbed a throw pillow and sat down on the edge of the couch.

Sarah tilted her head, studying me. "Just fine? Because it sounds like you've got a lot more than 'fine' going on in that brain of yours."

I tried to wave her off, but I could feel my cheeks getting warmer. "It's not that big of a deal. We just got tacos and went swimming. Normal summer stuff."

Sarah gave me a knowing smile, one eyebrow raised. "Uh-huh. Just normal 'fake date' stuff. And how's that whole fake-dating thing going, anyway?"

I glanced away, fidgeting with the edge of the pillow. "It's... weird, okay? Like, I don't know. Sometimes, it feels too easy. I mean, I'm supposed to be pretending with him, but it doesn't feel that way when we're actually together. Does that make any sense?"

Sarah laughed, setting her book aside and sitting up to face me. "It makes a lot of sense. Especially if you're starting to like him."

"What? No." I shook my head, but the word came out with absolutely zero conviction. "It's not... I don't know."

"Oh, please." Sarah gave me a teasing nudge. "You're totally into him. I've seen the way you look at him, especially at the bar when you kissed him. There's definitely something there."

I slumped back into the couch, covering my face with the pillow. "Okay, maybe I'm starting to like him… a little bit. Just a tiny bit."

"Tiny bit?" she asked, laughing softly. "You know I'm not going to let you get away with that. Tell me more!"

I peeked out from behind the pillow, hesitating before I continued. "It's just… the more time we spend together, the more I'm seeing this other side of him. The side that's actually… fun. And thoughtful. And… okay, really, really cute."

Sarah gave a triumphant grin. "See? I knew it. You're totally into him. And it's not even fake anymore, is it?"

"Ugh." I groaned, pressing my hands to my face again. "I don't know. I mean, it's still fake, technically. He probably doesn't even see it that way. He's just having fun messing with me, and I… I'm falling for it like a complete idiot."

Sarah shook her head, leaning in closer. "Rach, I saw the way he looked at you at the bar. You don't look at someone like that unless you're feeling something too. So maybe he's just as confused as you are."

"Maybe," I admitted softly. "But what if it's just all for show? What if he's only acting like this to keep up the whole 'pretend relationship' thing? I don't want to be the only one actually catching feelings."

Sarah reached over, squeezing my hand reassuringly. "You'll never know unless you let yourself feel what you're feeling. You don't have to dive in headfirst, but... maybe give yourself permission to enjoy it. See where things go."

I looked at her, a small smile tugging at my lips. "Yeah... maybe."

Sarah squeezed my hand once more before letting go, settling back on the couch. "Good. Now, keep me posted on every single detail. Especially the swoony ones."

I laughed, feeling a little lighter and a lot more hopeful. "Fine. But don't get too excited. This whole thing could still blow up in my face."

She shrugged, winking at me. "Maybe. Or maybe it'll turn out better than you ever expected."

* * *

The little bell above the café door jingled as we stepped into Driftwood Coffee House, a cozy, rustic place tucked just off the main road in town. The smell of espresso and fresh pastries wrapped around us like a warm hug, and I already felt myself relax.

Sarah made a beeline for the pastry case while Kyle scoped out a table by the window. I followed her, eyeing the cinnamon rolls the size of my head.

"I'm getting the lemon scone," Sarah announced, practically drooling. "What about you?"

I laughed. "Probably a dirty chai. I need the caffeine and the sugar."

While we waited in line, I glanced around at the hand-painted signs and beachy decor. It was the kind of place that felt like it had stories, like the walls themselves could tell you about the summer flings and quiet heartbreaks that had passed through.

Then I noticed the handwritten sign taped to the counter.

"Now Hiring - Summer help wanted! Barista & Front Counter. Inquire within."

My eyes lingered on it longer than I meant to.

Sarah noticed. "You should totally apply," she said, nudging me. "You're already a coffee addict. May as well get paid to be around it."

I hesitated. "I don't know..."

"Rachel," she said, turning to face me. "You've been going back and forth about staying in Tahoe all summer. This could be your sign."

Kyle joined us, carrying two iced lattes and a black coffee. "Sign for what?"

"She's applying for a job," Sarah said with a grin, before I could even open my mouth.

"I'm thinking about applying for a job," I corrected, but my heart was already racing.

I looked at the girl behind the counter—probably a few years younger than me, her ponytail messy and her smile warm. She handed a clipboard to someone on the other side of the bar.

Before I could lose my nerve, I stepped up. "Hey, uh… is the summer position still open?"

The girl lit up. "Yep! Want to fill out an application? I can grab one for you."

I nodded. "Yeah. I'd love that."

Sarah gave me a subtle thumbs-up behind her coffee, and Kyle raised his brows like he was impressed.

As I took the clipboard and a pen, I felt something shift—just a little. Like maybe I was starting to make this place feel like more than just a temporary stop.

6

Adam

The trolley rattled along the winding road, and I glanced over at Rachel beside me, her eyes fixed on the view outside the window. Sunlight filtered through the trees, dappling her face with soft shadows as she watched the passing scenery, her expression relaxed and curious. She was quieter than usual, and it gave me a strange sense of satisfaction, knowing I could surprise her with something she hadn't expected.

"You know, I still don't understand why you wouldn't just drive us there," she said, looking over at me with a slight smirk.

I shrugged, smirking back. "Where's the fun in that? Taking the trolley's part of the experience, Turner. Just sit back and enjoy the ride."

She shook her head, clearly amused, and leaned against the seat. We sat in comfortable silence as the trolley climbed up the switchbacks, weaving back and forth across the mountain. A few minutes later, the trolley came to a stop near the Emerald Bay overlook, and I stood up, reaching down to help her out of the seat. She hesitated before taking my hand, and I couldn't help but notice the slight blush that crept onto her cheeks as she let go.

We walked along the trail, weaving between groups of tourists and families taking photos of the bay below. The water was an unreal shade of blue-green, ringed by the dark silhouettes of the mountains, and Rachel's eyes lit up when she saw it. "Wow," she whispered, stepping closer to the edge of the lookout. "I've seen pictures, but it's different in person."

"Yeah," I said, feeling a strange sense of pride watching her take it in. "Nothing really compares to the real thing, does it?"

She nodded, looking genuinely awed. "Thanks for bringing me here."

I shrugged, trying to keep it casual. "Hey, I'm just making sure you get the full Tahoe experience. Can't come here and not hike down to the beach."

She grinned, her eyes sparkling as she looked over at me. "So, you're saying there's a hike involved?"

"Oh, yeah." I gave her a teasing grin. "Hope you're ready to work for that beach view."

Rachel narrowed her eyes, but she seemed excited, so we headed down the trail. The path wound through dense pine trees and rocky outcroppings, and I found myself slowing my usual pace to make sure she didn't stumble. She was determined, though, navigating the uneven ground without a word of complaint.

After about twenty minutes of hiking, we reached the bottom, where a small, rocky beach stretched along the shore. I tossed my backpack down, slipping off my shoes and walking right to the water's edge. Rachel followed, her eyes on the lake as she took in the view.

"Bet it's cold," I said, glancing at her. "But you can't say you hiked all the way down here and didn't go in."

She looked skeptical, glancing from me to the water. "Are you kidding? It's freezing."

"Come on, Turner. What's a little cold water?" I grinned, wading in a few steps, letting the icy lake lap up around my ankles. It was freezing, but I wasn't about to let her know that.

She rolled her eyes, kicking off her shoes and stepping carefully over the stones to join me. As soon as her toes touched the water, she gasped, pulling back with a shiver. "Okay, this is actual glacier water. You didn't mention that part."

I laughed, splashing a little water in her direction. "You'll get used to it."

She yelped, splashing back at me. "You're insane. I'm not getting in any deeper than this."

"Suit yourself." I shrugged, daring her with a playful look before I waded in farther until the water reached my knees. "But I'll be the one getting the best view."

She narrowed her eyes, watching me for a moment before she waded in, glaring at me the whole time. "You're impossible, you know that?"

"Maybe," I said, flashing her a grin. "But you're still here, aren't you?"

She splashed me again, laughing, and I found myself grinning like an idiot. She looked so carefree, the sun catching in her hair and making her eyes even brighter. For a second, I forgot we were supposed to be pretending. It felt real, being here with her, laughing over nothing, like we were just two people on a date, no expectations or weird history getting in the way.

When we finally retreated back to the beach, both of us shivering from the cold water, she dropped down onto the sand, leaning back on her hands as she looked out at the lake. I sat down beside her, feeling more at ease than I'd felt in a long time.

"This was a good idea," she said after a while, her voice soft. "I haven't had a day like this in... I don't know. It feels like forever."

I looked at her, something tugging at my chest. "Glad you're enjoying it."

She turned, meeting my gaze, and for a moment, the teasing and the pretending seemed to melt away. It was just us, sitting on the shore of a lake we both loved, sharing a moment I knew I'd probably replay in my mind a hundred times over.

But then, just as quickly, she looked away, picking up a small rock and tossing it into the water. "Thanks, Adam," she said, her voice light. "This was fun."

I nodded, trying to shake off the weird feeling in my chest. "Anytime, Turner."

We sat there in comfortable silence, watching the sun dip lower over the mountains, both of us pretending it was just another normal day, even though I was pretty sure we both knew better.

* * *

We made our way from the beach, climbing the path to the historic stone castle nestled at the head of Emerald Bay. Rachel walked beside me, her gaze bouncing between the lake views and the looming stone building with its turrets and Scandinavian architecture.

"Vikingsholm," she murmured, almost to herself. "It looks like it's straight out of a storybook."

I grinned, watching her take it all in. "Wait until you see the inside. You know, this place has been around since the 1920s. The woman who built it was a little eccentric—in the best way."

We approached the entrance, and a guide welcomed us, giving a brief overview of the tour. As we stepped into the stone-floored entry hall, Rachel leaned in closer to me, a fascinated smile tugging at her lips.

"I love the idea of someone just deciding, 'Hey, I want a Scandinavian castle right here in Tahoe,'" she whispered, eyes wide. "This is kind of amazing."

The guide began to describe the structure, pointing out the Scandinavian wood carvings, intricate ironwork, and stone arches as we moved through the dimly lit rooms.

Rachel and I lingered at the back of the group, and I watched her soak it all in, her expression shifting from interest to wonder.

When we entered the living room, she nudged me. "Did you know the woman who built this place actually had authentic materials shipped from Scandinavia? This isn't just a replica—it's the real deal."

"Someone did her research," I teased, smirking as she shot me a quick look.

"Hey, I might have looked it up on the way here," she admitted, her cheeks coloring a little. "I wanted to know what I was getting myself into. Plus, I didn't want you to one-up me with your tour guide trivia."

I laughed. "Well, I'm impressed. You're taking the fake date duties pretty seriously."

She shrugged, giving me a playful smile. "I aim to please."

We wandered into the dining hall, where the walls were lined with timber beams and small diamond-shaped windows let in slants of light that fell across the table. The guide explained that the intricate woodwork had been done by hand, and Rachel stepped closer, brushing her fingers across the carved surface with awe.

"It must have taken years to build this place," she whispered, her voice full of admiration.

"Yeah, it did," I said, moving beside her. "You know, I used to come here as a kid on field trips, but it's been years since I've really looked at it. Kind of forgot how impressive it is."

She looked up at me, a small smile on her lips. "Thanks for bringing me here, Adam. I didn't know I'd be this into it, but it's… it's special."

I felt my chest tighten, that familiar feeling that had been creeping in for days whenever I looked at her. "I'm glad you're enjoying it," I said, keeping my voice light. "Not every day I bring a girl to see a castle, you know."

"Oh, really?" she said, raising an eyebrow, the corners of her mouth turning up. "So this is a rare Adam Harrison treat?"

"Something like that," I muttered, trying to ignore the way she was looking at me, like maybe she was seeing more than just my usual laid-back attitude.

The tour continued through smaller, cozier rooms—the bedrooms, a narrow spiral staircase, and a small library lined with shelves of old books. When we reached a sunlit alcove with a cushioned window seat that overlooked the bay, Rachel stopped, her eyes lighting up.

"This is my favorite room," she whispered, glancing back at me. "Can you imagine waking up to this view every day?"

I followed her gaze out the window, where the bay stretched out in shades of deep blue and green, sunlight glinting off the water. "I don't know. I think I'd get too attached, and I'd never leave."

She chuckled, sitting on the window seat and gazing out at the water. "Maybe that wouldn't be so bad. A view like this might be worth it."

I sat down beside her, close enough that our knees almost touched, and we both looked out over the bay. The other people on the tour had moved into the next room, leaving us in a rare, quiet moment.

"So, if you could live anywhere, where would it be?" I asked, watching her expression.

She thought about it, a soft smile playing on her lips. "I don't know. I've always been drawn to the mountains, places with lakes and trees and endless sky. Like this."

"You're in the right place, then," I said, feeling a pang of something I couldn't name. "Tahoe seems to suit you."

She laughed lightly. "I guess it does, for now. But I always thought I'd end up somewhere bigger, like New York. I used to picture myself in a city, where everything is alive and buzzing."

"New York?" I said, a little surprised. "That doesn't exactly seem like you."

She tilted her head, considering. "No, maybe not. I guess I don't really know what I want yet."

The room grew quiet, just the faint sound of the wind rustling through the trees outside. I could feel the warmth radiating from her arm, close enough that if I moved just a few inches, we'd be touching.

"I think you'll figure it out," I said, my voice softer than I intended. "You're one of the most determined people I know. You'll end up exactly where you're meant to be."

She looked at me then, her eyes lingering on mine, and for a second, I almost forgot we were just pretending. This whole arrangement, this plan to make everyone think we were together—it all felt like a distant joke. Because, sitting here in a castle by the lake, it didn't feel fake at all.

"Thank you," she whispered, her voice barely audible.

The spell broke when we heard footsteps echoing in the hall, and we both turned, snapping out of whatever moment we'd just had. She stood, smoothing her hands over her clothes and giving me a small, shy smile.

“So,” she said, back to her playful tone. “What’s next on this very ‘rare Adam Harrison tour’?”

I grinned, stuffing my hands in my pockets as we rejoined the group. “Guess you’ll have to stick around and find out.”

As we continued the tour, though, I couldn’t shake the feeling that something had shifted between us—something I couldn’t take back, even if I wanted to.

* * *

The water was calm as we paddled out, our kayaks cutting through the deep blue surface with steady strokes. Rachel was a few feet ahead of me, her ponytail bouncing with each pull on her paddle as we made our way toward Fannette Island, the small rocky island that rose like a lone outpost in the middle of the bay.

"How am I beating you, Adam?" she called over her shoulder, glancing back with a grin. Her voice carried across the water, teasing, with that edge that always got under my skin in the best way.

"Just letting you think you’re winning," I shot back, digging my paddle in and quickening my pace to catch up.

"Sure you are." She rolled her eyes, her grin widening, and I couldn't help but chuckle. She had no idea just how much I loved getting a rise out of her.

A few minutes later, we reached the island, beaching our kayaks on the narrow strip of shoreline. The old stone ruins of the tea house sat at the highest point, overlooking the entire bay. It was deserted, quiet except for the gentle lap of the lake against the rocks. Rachel took a few steps, looking around in awe.

"It's beautiful up here," she said, her voice softening as she took in the view.

"Best seat in the house," I agreed, watching her. "But wait 'til you see it from the water."

She glanced at me, raising an eyebrow. "You mean from jumping off the cliffs into the water?"

I smirked, tilting my head toward the edge of the island where the rocks dropped off sharply. "You up for it?"

She crossed her arms, giving me a look like she was considering backing out, but I could see that glint of excitement in her eyes. "Are you?"

"Oh, I'm in," I said, already kicking off my shoes and pulling my shirt over my head. I caught her staring at me for a split second before she looked away, and I fought the urge to smirk. I knew she'd take the dare if I did it first.

"Fine," she said, giving me a challenging look as she slipped out of her shoes and set her bag on the ground. "But don't chicken out halfway down."

"You think I'd chicken out?"

She shrugged, a teasing smile on her lips. "I just know how you are, Harrison."

I laughed, striding over to the edge and looking down at the water, which glimmered a good fifteen feet below. The drop was exhilarating, the kind that made your stomach flip right before you leaped. "On three?" I called, nodding for her to join me.

She stepped up beside me, glancing down nervously before giving me a determined look. "Fine. Three... two..."

Before she could finish counting, I leapt, throwing myself off the edge and letting out a loud whoop as I plummeted toward the lake. The cold water hit like an electric shock, but the thrill of the jump left me grinning as I surfaced, shaking the water from my hair.

When I looked up, Rachel was standing on the ledge, hands on her hips, glaring down at me. "Didn't even let me get to one, did you?"

"Just had to make sure you didn't back out," I called, laughing.

She huffed, took a deep breath, and then finally jumped, letting out a surprised yelp as she fell. She hit the water with a splash, disappearing beneath the surface before popping up a few feet away, sputtering and laughing at the same time.

"That was... ridiculous!" she said, pushing her wet hair back from her face as she tried to catch her breath.

"Good ridiculous or bad ridiculous?" I asked, drifting closer as we treaded water.

She splashed me. "Good, but you're still a jerk for jumping first."

"Maybe," I said, laughing as I splashed her back. "But you were never actually going to back out, were you?"

She rolled her eyes, but she was smiling, and for a second, I forgot about the whole fake relationship thing. Here, in the water with her, it felt real. Like we were just two people having fun, not playing a part.

We swam for a while, drifting close to the island's rocky edge, occasionally glancing back at the view. Eventually, Rachel floated on her back, staring up at the blue sky, her face lit by the sun. I drifted beside her, the silence between us comfortable.

"You know," she said quietly, "I didn't think I'd have this much fun back here. I figured this summer would be all family obligations and awkward reunions."

"Is that what I am?" I asked, grinning. "An awkward reunion?"

She laughed, turning to face me, her eyes sparkling. "Sometimes. But sometimes, you're actually not so bad."

I pretended to be offended, clutching my chest. "Not so bad? High praise, Turner."

She rolled her eyes, swimming a few feet away before glancing back, her gaze softening. "No, I mean it. I'm... glad you're here this summer."

Something about the way she said it, with that rare vulnerability, made me pause. I swam closer, the space between us shrinking until I could see every sunlit freckle on her face.

"Me too," I murmured, the words coming out before I could stop them.

For a second, we just looked at each other, and I wondered if she was feeling it too—that strange, quiet pull that was making me forget this was all pretend. But then she looked away, swimming back toward the island, and I let her go, pushing down whatever I'd felt in that moment.

"Race you back to the kayaks," she called, a hint of her usual teasing edge returning.

"Loser buys the next round of tacos," I shot back, grinning as I kicked off toward shore, refusing to look too deeply at the way my heart was pounding.

Because deep down, I knew that every time I let myself get closer to her, it felt a little more real—and that was something I wasn't sure I was ready to face.

7

Rachel

I was already sitting on the front porch of Adam's cabin when he pulled up, the bag of cookies I'd made for him sitting beside me, the warm, familiar scent of chocolate chip and caramel filling the air. As soon as he saw me, he waved, a smile pulling at his lips.

"You made it just in time," I called out, grinning at him. "I was about to start without you."

"I'm not so easily replaced, Turner," he said, stepping up onto the porch. "I would've noticed if you ate all the cookies."

"I could've," I teased. "But I'm generous."

He laughed, opening the door and stepping aside so I could enter. The cabin was cozy, with a rustic charm I loved. It had that cabin smell—the mix of pine and the faint scent of the lake that I found comforting. Adam's living room was mostly one open space, with old leather couches and a stone fireplace, the walls lined with shelves full of movies. It was exactly what I would expect from him—chilled, but with a sense of personality.

"So, what's it gonna be?" Adam asked, scanning his movie collection. "Action? Rom-com? Something so bad it's good?"

I couldn't help but raise an eyebrow. "You have rom-coms? You, of all people?"

He gave me an exaggerated shrug, clearly unbothered by my teasing. "Gotta have something for all occasions."

I rolled my eyes, but I couldn't help but laugh. "Fine. Surprise me. Just no horror movies, okay? I'm not in the mood to be scared out of my mind."

"I can do that," he said, his voice light, but I could see the mischievous gleam in his eyes as he pulled a DVD from the shelf. Twilight—classic, and it felt just right. I sat on the couch, adjusting the blanket around my shoulders as Adam slid the DVD into the player.

"Are you sure I'm not going to regret this?" I asked as I shifted into a more comfortable position on the couch, opening the bag of cookies and offering him one.

"No regrets," he said, grinning as he grabbed one. "Though I do warn you, my movie taste is impeccable."

"Oh, I'm sure," I said, taking a cookie. "I'm only trusting you because of the cookies."

We both leaned back into the couch as the opening credits rolled. The movie started, and we settled into the rhythm of our usual banter—commenting on the absurdly dramatic moments and making fun of the cheesy dialogue. Adam's voice would drop a few decibels when something particularly ridiculous happened, and I'd glance over to find him grinning at me, clearly enjoying the fact that we were both on the same page.

But as the movie progressed, I couldn't help but notice the way Adam kept edging closer to me. At first, it was subtle—his knee just brushing mine, then his arm resting on the back of the couch. But before I knew it, his shoulder was pressed against mine, and I was acutely aware of the warmth of his skin against mine. The space between us felt like it was shrinking, and when his arm nudged mine, I didn't pull away.

"Is this okay?" he asked quietly, glancing at me, almost uncertain.

"Yeah," I murmured, my voice barely above a whisper. "It's fine."

I wasn't sure if I was telling the truth, though. My heart was beating just a little faster, and there was a small, unfamiliar flutter in my chest that I wasn't sure how to place. I'd always been able to joke with Adam, but this... this felt different.

The movie played on, but I wasn't paying much attention anymore. I could feel the heat radiating off of him, I could smell the faint musk of his cologne mixed with the fresh scent of the outdoors. It made me hyper-aware of the space we shared on the couch. His arm, resting along the back, was close enough that I could feel the tension in the air between us, and I couldn't decide whether it was because we were both pretending—*playing* this fake couple—or because I was starting to like this, starting to like him, in a way I wasn't ready to admit.

We sat in silence for a long stretch, neither of us speaking, just watching the movie. But every now and then, I'd catch him glancing at me, and I'd feel this strange pull toward him, like I was tethered to him by some invisible thread.

When the movie ended, I realized I hadn't even noticed the last half of it. All I could think about was how close we'd gotten, how easy it had been to slip into this space between us that felt so normal, despite knowing it wasn't. I shifted, running a hand through my hair, not sure what to say.

"So..." I began, trying to fill the silence with something light, "what else do you have in this macho collection of yours?"

He grinned, clearly not wanting to let the moment slip away. "Oh, I've got *plenty* of movies. But you keep making fun of me, and I might just put on the worst horror flick I can find."

"Please, no," I said, laughing. "I didn't sign up for that."

He leaned forward and grabbed another movie, but I couldn't shake the feeling that there was something else hanging in the air between us. I glanced up at him, and for a brief second, it felt like we were standing on the edge of something neither of us was ready to face.

But instead of acknowledging it, Adam just reached for the blanket and tossed it over his lap with a wink. "Alright, no horror. I'll spare you."

I smiled back, my stomach fluttering again, but this time I couldn't brush it off. I wasn't sure where this was going, but with every passing moment, it felt more real—this connection, this *thing* between us. But just like before, I didn't know what it was.

We ended up putting on another lighthearted movie, but I couldn't help but notice the way he settled beside me again, how his shoulder brushed mine, how comfortable we were together, even though we both knew we shouldn't be.

That fake relationship was getting harder to fake with every passing moment.

* * *

The sun was just starting to set as I sat at the kitchen table, the glow of my laptop screen illuminating my face. The quiet hum of the cabin was soothing, the familiar sound of the lake lapping against the shore drifting in through the open window. It was the kind of peace I'd been craving for months—yet all I could think about was the knot in my stomach, the one that seemed to tighten every time I clicked on a new job listing.

I had to face it. Summer was winding down, and as much as I liked the idea of sticking around Tahoe forever, reality was creeping in. The fall was just around the corner, and I needed a job. A real job. The kind that came with a paycheck and responsibilities, the kind that would launch me into my life after graduation. And that meant applying for jobs back home in Oregon.

I scrolled through job postings, my mind wandering, but no matter how many resumes I sent out or cover letters I typed, my thoughts kept drifting to him.

Adam.

It had started off as a joke—a silly, fake relationship to keep our families from asking too many questions. But with each day, each date, each moment where we slipped into our roles a little too easily, the line between real and pretend blurred. It didn't help that we kept having moments that felt real. Like last night, when we were on the couch together, watching a movie. Or when we went kayaking at Emerald Bay, laughing over the fact that neither of us knew what we were doing, yet somehow it felt like we'd done it a thousand times before.

I couldn't stop thinking about the way his hand brushed against mine on the trolley ride, or how easy it was to laugh with him, to tease him and be teased in return. How his smile made my heart do that funny little dance, the kind that I didn't want to admit.

The truth was, the more time I spent with Adam, the harder it was to remember that none of this was real. That we were faking it for the summer, a summer romance that would disappear once the leaves changed color and we went back to our separate lives.

I shook my head, forcing my attention back to the screen. I had to focus. I couldn't let myself get sidetracked. There was no future here for me—no future with Adam, no matter how much I enjoyed our time together.

But the thought of leaving this place, of leaving him, twisted something inside me. I had a life to go back to in Oregon—friends, a career I was ready to start, my own apartment. There was nothing here that was permanent, nothing here that wasn't just a summer fling. That's what I had to remind myself. We were pretending, and it wasn't real.

The cursor blinked on the job application page, the questions waiting for me to fill them out. I clicked through a few more listings, but I could hardly concentrate. I could feel the weight of everything unspoken between Adam and me, the quiet pull I was trying to ignore.

It had to stay fake. Because if it didn't, if it turned into something real, I wasn't sure I was ready for that kind of change. I wasn't sure I wanted to let go of what I was already comfortable with—the safe, easy relationship we had built in our little bubble.

But then I thought about him again. The way he smiled when he looked at me. The way he made me laugh, even when he was being obnoxious. The way he was always there when I needed him.

I exhaled sharply, feeling the weight of everything pressing down on me. If I let myself feel too much, if I let this thing with Adam get too real, it was going to make leaving that much harder.

I closed the laptop, staring at the darkened screen. No use applying to more jobs tonight. My mind was elsewhere. With him.

I stood up and walked to the window, looking out over the lake. The evening sky was fading into shades of purple and orange, the water reflecting the last bits of sunlight. I felt like I was caught between two worlds—between what I had to do and what I was feeling.

And no matter how hard I tried to push those feelings aside, I couldn't deny that part of me didn't want this summer to end. Not just because of the lake or the cabin, but because of him.

I sighed, rubbing my temples, wishing I could stop thinking about him. But Adam Harrison was impossible to forget.

* * *

The phone felt heavier than usual in my hand as I dialed Carissa's number. I hadn't talked to her in a few days, and I needed someone to talk to—someone who wasn't physically here, someone who would give me an honest, unbiased opinion about what was going on with Adam.

The phone rang a few times before she picked up. "Rachel! Hey!" Carissa's voice was warm and upbeat, as always. "How's the cabin life treating you?"

I smiled as I flopped back onto the couch. "It's… it's good, actually. Really good."

"That's great! So, you're surviving the time with Sarah and Kyle?"

"Barely." I laughed. "But there's more going on than just family. I need to tell you something."

There was a pause on the other end. "Ooh, that sounds serious. Spill it."

I hesitated for a moment, the words sitting on the tip of my tongue. It wasn't like I'd never told Carissa everything—she was my best friend. But talking about Adam felt… complicated. I wasn't sure how to even explain it.

"I've—well, I've been spending a lot of time with someone here. Someone who… isn't exactly new to me." I bit my lip, trying to figure out how to phrase this. "His name's Adam Harrison. You know him. We grew up together, but we hated each other back then. He's my childhood enemy, basically."

Carissa's voice was incredulous. "Wait. Hold on. Adam Harrison? You mean the guy who used to steal your lunch at summer camp and make fun of you for your terrible karaoke choices?"

I laughed, though it felt like a nervous laugh. "That's him. Yeah. I know. You'd think I'd learned my lesson by now, right?"

She let out a dramatic sigh. "Oh, Rachel. This is going to be good. But, go on. What's happening with him?"

I took a deep breath. "Well, here's the thing. We've been pretending to date for the past few weeks. It's... it's a long story, but we both needed an excuse to get our families off our backs. So, we made up this whole fake relationship. But... it's starting to feel real. And I don't know what to do with that."

I could practically hear Carissa sitting up straighter on the other end of the line. "Wait, wait, wait. You're saying that this thing you've got going with Mr. Lunch-Stealer-Adam Harrison is starting to feel real? Like, *real* real?"

"Yeah," I sighed. "I don't know how it happened. One minute, it was all jokes and fake dates, and the next, I'm looking at him like he's... well, not a joke anymore. I'm starting to like him, Carissa."

"Holy crap, Rachel." She laughed, a knowing laugh that I could almost picture. "I mean, I've seen you both together on social media, and you guys *look* cute. But I didn't know it was going this far. What's the problem? Why are you freaking out?"

"I just..." I ran a hand through my hair, feeling the weight of the situation. "I'm leaving at the end of the summer. I've got to go back to Oregon, get my life together. It's not like I can stay here, even if this is real. He's not... He's not the kind of guy I want to make big decisions with, you know?"

"I don't know." Carissa's voice softened, the teasing tone replaced by something more sincere. "Maybe it's worth considering. I mean, I get that it's a summer fling, but it doesn't have to stay that way, right? You don't have to figure everything out right now. You're here, and he's here. So, why not just see where it goes? Maybe you're more ready for something real than you think."

"I don't know if I am," I admitted. "It feels like I'm rushing into something, and I don't want to mess things up."

"Rachel, when have you not rushed into something? You know you're the queen of impulsive decisions." She paused, and I could hear the grin in her voice. "But this one? Maybe it's the right kind of impulsive. You've been stuck in this weird limbo since graduation. Maybe this is what you need to take that step forward. And Adam? You've known him forever. You've got a history with him. If he's starting to mean more to you than just a summer distraction, you need to go for it. Don't overthink it."

I felt my chest tighten as I processed her words. Was she right? Was this real? Was it something worth giving a shot, even if it meant I'd be leaving in a few weeks?

"I don't know, Carissa," I said quietly. "What if it's just a summer thing, like we said? What if I get too attached and then leave and it all falls apart?"

"You don't know it's just a summer thing yet, Rach. And even if it is, you deserve to have something good right now. Maybe it'll be short and sweet. But maybe it'll be something more. You'll never know unless you try."

I sat back on the couch, staring out at the lake, the golden light of the setting sun dancing on the water. Maybe she was right. Maybe I was overthinking it. Maybe it was okay to take a chance on something real for once.

"Okay, fine. Maybe I will," I said with a small smile. "But only if you promise not to judge me if I completely mess this up."

"I'm not promising that," Carissa replied, her tone teasing once again. "But if you do mess it up, I'll be here to help you fix it. And we'll have a hell of a story to tell when it's over."

I laughed. "Deal. Thanks, Carissa. I needed to hear that."

"Anytime. Just don't forget, you're allowed to be happy, okay? Don't let yourself walk away from something that could be great."

I ended the call, leaning back against the couch with a sigh. She was right. I didn't know what was going to happen with Adam, but maybe I needed to stop overthinking and just enjoy what was in front of me.

* * *

My phone buzzed just as I stepped out of the shower, and I wrapped a towel around me, dripping onto the tile as I fumbled for it on the sink.

Unknown Number.

I hesitated, then swiped to answer. "Hello?"

"Hi, is this Rachel Turner?"

"Yes, this is she."

"Hey Rachel, this is Lindsey from Driftwood Coffee House. I just wanted to let you know—we'd love to offer you the summer position, if you're still interested."

My heart leapt. I sat on the edge of the tub, still wet and wrapped in my towel, suddenly grinning like an idiot.

"Yes, I'm definitely still interested! Thank you so much."

She gave me the details—start date, training times, what to wear—and by the time I hung up, I was practically buzzing.

I got dressed quickly and grabbed my keys, barely giving myself time to dry my hair. I had to tell Adam.

He was out back at his place, shirtless and hosing off the patio. His hair was a little messy, the late afternoon sun catching in the golden ends. I tried to be casual as I walked up, but my smile gave me away.

He turned at the sound of my steps and grinned. "Hey, sunshine. You look like you just won the lottery."

"Better," I said. "I got the job."

He dropped the hose and walked over, a surprised and happy look on his face. "You did?"

"Yep." I tried to play it cool, but my excitement spilled out. "Driftwood called this morning. I start next week."

Adam raised his brows, wiping his hands on his jeans. "So this means..."

"That I'm staying. At least for the summer." I paused, watching his face carefully.

His expression softened in a way that made my stomach flutter. He stepped closer, brushing a wet strand of hair away from my cheek.

"That's great news," he replied. "You know that means you have to start paying for our fake dates, right?"

"Haha, you wish," I said with a big grin, turning on my heels to walk back inside.

This summer was turning out to be better than I expected. Maybe even in ways I didn't quite anticipate.

8

Adam

The engine of the jet ski roared to life beneath me as I revved the throttle, the water spraying up behind us in a wild burst. I glanced over at Rachel, who was gripping the handlebars of her own jet ski, her eyes wide and a grin spreading across her face.

"You ready for this?" I shouted, my voice barely cutting through the wind whipping around us.

She shot me a challenging look, her hair flying behind her like a wild streak of dark silk. "You're going to regret underestimating me, Harrison!"

I chuckled, giving my jet ski another burst of speed as I zoomed ahead, leaving a trail of frothy waves in my wake. I couldn't help but tease her. That's what I did. It's how we worked, and I liked it. But something about today—something about her—felt different. The usual easy banter between us had been there all day, but there was an edge to it now. Every touch, every glance, every laugh felt like more. I wasn't sure if it was just because we were spending so much time together, or if the whole "pretend relationship" thing was making me think too much. Either way, it felt like the lines between fake and real were starting to blur, and I wasn't sure I was ready to figure out which side I was on.

"Come on, slowpoke!" Rachel yelled, pulling up alongside me.

I couldn't help it—I laughed. She was really good at this, despite her teasing. We'd been out here for hours, zipping across the lake, each of us trying to outdo the other. I'd been all talk at first, thinking I'd show her how it was done, but she'd quickly proven she could handle herself just fine.

"Okay, you win. I'll admit it," I called out, raising my hands in mock surrender. "You're better than me. But I did teach you everything you know!"

She shot me a look of mock disbelief, her grin widening. "Really? Because I remember you getting stuck in the reeds over by the point."

"Don't you dare bring that up," I shot back, laughing as I steered my jet ski back toward her. "That was a one-time accident, and I'll have you know, I deliberately chose the path less traveled."

She snorted, then pulled ahead of me again, laughing as she cut across the water, the spray rising around her. I watched her for a moment, the sunlight dancing on the surface of the lake, catching the streaks of her blonde hair, the sparkle in her eyes. There was something about the way she looked right now—so carefree, so alive—that made my chest tighten.

She was supposed to be a summer fling, right? A fake girlfriend. Nothing more than a distraction to keep the family off our backs. But the more I spent time with her, the more I couldn't shake the feeling that there was something real between us. I just didn't know how to deal with it.

We slowed down, both of us idling side by side in the middle of the lake, letting the waves rock us gently.

"Not bad for someone who was terrified of getting wet earlier," I teased.

"Shut up," she replied, but there was a softness to her tone. She reached over and splashed me with a quick burst of water, laughing as I scrambled to wipe it out of my eyes.

"You're ruthless," I said with a grin, still wiping my face.

"Gotta keep you on your toes, Harrison."

We hovered in silence for a moment, just letting the water settle, the hum of the engines the only sound. I glanced over at her again, the distance between us feeling like nothing.

"You know," I said after a moment, my voice quieter than before, "I'm kind of glad you're here this summer."

She raised an eyebrow, clearly not expecting the shift in tone. "Oh yeah? Glad to be stuck with me for the next few weeks?"

I laughed, though it was a little strained. "Well, not *stuck*... but yeah. I'm glad. It's... it's nice having someone to hang out with. Someone I can count on."

Her eyes softened for a second, and then she shrugged, like she hadn't noticed the change in the air. "I'm glad too, I guess. I wasn't sure what I was expecting when I got here, but it's been... fun."

I couldn't help but smile at that, even though there was a tightness in my chest. It was like we were both pretending everything was fine, pretending we hadn't crossed a line or two already. But neither of us was willing to admit it, not yet.

"I was thinking," I said, trying to push down the feeling that was crawling up my throat, "maybe we should go out to the point after this. There's a place up there with some good food. I'll buy you lunch."

She turned to me, her expression more serious now, as though she were reading between the lines of my words. "I'm just your fake girlfriend, Adam. We're just pretending to be dating, right? I mean, it's not like we're a couple. I can pay for myself."

The words stung, even though I knew they were just the truth. But something in the way she said it—like she was already distancing herself—hit me harder than I expected.

"Right," I said, trying to keep the bitterness out of my voice. "We're just hanging out. No big deal."

She stared at me for a moment, and I could see that look in her eyes—the one that told me she didn't believe what she was saying either.

It was starting to feel real, whether either of us was ready to admit it or not.

I started the engine again, my thoughts a little jumbled as I looked over at her. "Come on. Let's go get lunch before you beat me at jet skiing again."

Rachel grinned, her usual playful self coming back. "Oh, you know I'm going to win."

"Not if I have anything to say about it," I said, revving the throttle and taking off once again, the sound of her jet ski roaring behind me.

But even as I zoomed ahead, the words she'd said still lingered in my mind.

It wasn't just pretend anymore. Not for me.

And I wasn't sure how much longer I could keep pretending it was.

* * *

The small lakeside restaurant had a rustic charm, with wooden beams and open windows offering a perfect view of the sparkling lake. We sat at a table near the water, the soft breeze carrying the scent of fresh air and grilling burgers. It was the kind of place that made you feel like summer was alive and well, and yet, as I looked across the table at Rachel, the lightheartedness of the moment seemed a little out of reach.

Rachel flipped through the menu with her usual focus, her brow furrowed in determination. She looked completely at ease—like she always did. But I wasn't. Not right now. Not after what she'd said earlier.

The words still echoed in my head: "We're just pretending to be dating."

It had hurt more than I expected, and even now, as she scanned the menu like she didn't have a care in the world, I couldn't shake the sting. This was supposed to be temporary, right? A way to fool our families, nothing more. But somewhere along the way, I'd let myself believe that maybe it could be more than that. Maybe we could be more.

But clearly, Rachel didn't feel the same.

She looked up from the menu and smiled. "You ready to order? The burgers here are supposed to be amazing."

I forced a smile, pushing my thoughts aside. "Yeah, I'll have the cheeseburger with extra bacon. And a beer, if they have it."

Rachel raised an eyebrow. "You sure? It's only noon, you know."

I shrugged, trying to brush off the awkward tension that had settled between us. "What can I say? I'm on the lake. Doesn't seem too early for a beer."

She laughed, the sound light and carefree, and I wondered if she even realized how off-balance I felt. I wasn't sure if I could keep pretending that this whole thing was as casual as we both wanted it to be.

"I'll just have a regular burger, no cheese, and a lemonade," she said, handing the menu to the waitress who had just arrived.

As soon as the waitress left, the silence stretched between us, and I couldn't stand it. I had to say something. We can't keep pretending this is nothing, I thought. But the words stuck in my throat, and all I could do was stare at my drink, tapping my fingers on the glass.

"So," I began, my voice sounding rougher than I meant, "you really think this is just fake? That's all it is?"

Rachel's gaze flickered up to meet mine. "What do you mean?" she asked, clearly a little caught off guard.

"I mean, that's what you said earlier," I pressed, not wanting to let it go. "That we're just pretending. Just hanging out, nothing more."

She seemed to hesitate for a moment, then shrugged, looking down at her napkin. "Well, isn't it? I mean, that's how we started, right? We're just faking it for our families. I thought we both knew that."

The words hit harder than I expected. I had known it was temporary. I had known it wasn't supposed to be real. But hearing her say it so plainly—like there was no possibility for anything else—made my chest tighten.

"Right," I said, trying to sound like I wasn't bothered. "Just a fling. Nothing more."

I could hear the slight bitterness in my own voice, and I immediately regretted it. But the truth was, her words had made me feel like a fool. Like I'd been kidding myself all along.

Rachel shifted in her seat, a small frown forming between her brows. "Adam, it's not that I don't like spending time with you, or that I don't enjoy this... whatever this is. I just don't want to pretend it's anything more than a summer thing." She paused, biting her lip. "That's what we agreed on, right?"

Her words stung, and I tried to hide it, pretending to focus on the lake outside. The truth was, I hadn't agreed to that. Not entirely. Not when I felt like this.

But I nodded, playing it off. "Yeah. Right. Summer fling."

She looked at me for a second, then sighed, as if she could sense the tension building between us. "I just... I don't want things to get weird, Adam. I'm not saying we can't have fun, but I think we both know this isn't going anywhere. You know?"

I forced a smile, but it didn't quite reach my eyes. "Yeah. I know."

The waitress brought our burgers, setting them down in front of us. I picked up my burger and took a bite, trying to distract myself from the heaviness in my chest. It tasted good—juicy, smoky, just what I needed—but the flavor didn't quite fill the hole I felt now. The words I had said, and the ones she had said in return, kept spinning in my head.

Rachel took a bite of her burger, and I watched her, wondering if she could tell how much this was bothering me. Could she see through the facade I was putting on?

"So, uh," I said, trying to shift the mood, "I guess we're still doing this whole pretend thing, right? For our families?"

"Yeah," she said, but there was a softness in her tone now. "We'll keep going with it. I mean, it's working, isn't it?"

I nodded, but inside, I wasn't sure if I was pretending anymore. And if I wasn't—if this thing between us was more real than either of us was willing to admit—I wasn't sure where that left us.

The rest of the lunch passed in relative silence, both of us chewing on our words more than the food in front of us. As we finished up and the waitress brought the check, I couldn't help but wonder how much longer I could keep pretending everything was fine.

Because right now, it didn't feel fine. Not at all.

9

Rachel

The evening air had cooled as we made our way down the winding path to the beach at Sand Harbor, the soft crunch of gravel underfoot the only sound as we walked in silence. The sun was setting, casting a golden glow over the water and turning the sky into a painter's palette of pinks and oranges. Kids were jumping off the large rocks into the deep lake water, sending splashes of water into the colorful sky. The atmosphere was perfect for a night out—romantic, picturesque. But the tension between Adam and me felt anything but.

I stole a glance at him, walking beside me with his usual easy stride, but there was something off in his expression. He had his hands shoved into the pockets of his jeans, his jaw tight in a way I'd seen before when he was frustrated, but trying not to show it.

He hadn't said much since our conversation earlier. The one where I had casually mentioned how our "relationship" was just for show, and he'd brushed it off like it was no big deal. But I knew it was bothering him. The way his smile had faltered, the way he'd grown quieter afterward, made it clear that my words had hit a nerve.

I wasn't sure why it bothered me now. We'd always agreed that this whole thing was just for the summer, just something to keep our families off our backs. But now, with Adam by my side, I was starting to feel like maybe I wasn't as indifferent about it as I had once thought. And it wasn't just about what we were doing—it was about how *he* made me feel.

"Are you going to talk to me, or are we just going to keep walking in silence?" I asked, trying to break the awkwardness that seemed to hang between us like a thick fog.

Adam glanced at me briefly before looking away. "What do you want me to say?" His voice was cool, but I could hear the edge beneath it. He had clearly been stewing over the whole thing.

I bit my lip, regretting the way I'd phrased things earlier. But at the same time, I wasn't sure how to fix it now. I had called it a "fake relationship," and that word had somehow stuck. "I didn't mean it like that," I said softly, feeling the sting of my own words echoing in the space between us.

Adam stopped walking for a moment, and I turned to face him. The anger in his eyes was gone, but there was something else there. Something guarded. "You don't think I know what you meant?" he asked, his voice low. "I get it, Rachel. It's fine."

I wasn't sure if he was trying to convince me or himself. It didn't sound fine. And the way his hands tightened into fists as he spoke made it clear that it wasn't.

"You're still upset," I said, crossing my arms over my chest, suddenly feeling defensive. "Look, we agreed this wasn't anything serious. That it was just for the summer. Why does it bother you so much?"

He hesitated for a long moment before letting out a frustrated sigh. "Because, maybe I don't want to just pretend anymore. Maybe I don't want to keep acting like it's all some joke, Rachel." He turned away, clearly trying to hide the frustration that had now taken over his face.

I was taken aback by his words. "You think it's a joke?" I couldn't hide the surprise in my voice. "Adam, we're not supposed to be doing this. It's just... temporary. We're not supposed to—"

"I know," he interrupted, his voice barely above a whisper, his back still to me. "But sometimes it feels... real. And that's not what we signed up for, is it?" He turned to face me, his expression hard. "Because I didn't sign up for this to feel real."

I swallowed hard. The words I had said to him earlier echoed in my mind. "Fake relationship." I had brushed it off like it didn't matter, but now it did. I could see it in his eyes—this mattered.

"Look," I said, stepping closer, trying to make him understand. "I didn't mean to hurt you. I just... I didn't know how to explain it any other way. But you're right. It's not a joke. It's not something I want to treat lightly, either. But that's what this is, right? A temporary thing. Just for the summer."

His gaze softened, but there was still a guarded look in his eyes. "Right. Temporary."

We stood there for a moment, the tension still lingering between us, but now more unspoken. The faint sound of waves crashing against the shore seemed far away as I tried to process everything I was feeling. I didn't know what this was anymore—whether it was just two people pretending for the sake of others, or something more complicated that neither of us had been prepared for.

Finally, Adam broke the silence. "Let's just... enjoy tonight, okay? No more talking about it." His voice was quieter now, like he had given up on trying to make sense of it all. "We're here for the ballet. Let's just be here."

I nodded, feeling a pang of guilt, but also a strange sense of relief. The last thing I wanted was to ruin the evening by dwelling on things that couldn't be fixed so easily. Still, as we approached Sarah and Kyle, the weight of our conversation didn't entirely fade. It was there—between us, under the surface, like the murky water that lapped at the edge of the beach.

I smiled weakly at Sarah and Kyle as we sat down on our chairs. Sarah, as usual, was all smiles, clearly excited for the show. Kyle offered us some snacks, and we settled in, the ballet set to begin soon.

But as I glanced at Adam, sitting beside me, I couldn't ignore the fact that things weren't as simple as they had seemed before. The moment between us had shifted. And no matter how much I tried to pretend otherwise, I couldn't deny that something had changed.

The soft hum of the crowd faded as the stage lights illuminated the wooden platform against the backdrop of the lake. The sound of gentle waves crashing on the shore seemed to slow, almost as if the world around us had paused. I took a deep breath, trying to shake off the tension that had settled between Adam and me, and focused on the performance about to begin.

The first dancer appeared, her silhouette framed by the soft pink light of the setting sun. She wore a delicate costume that shimmered in the evening light, a pale, almost ethereal blue that looked like it had been pulled straight from the sky. She stepped lightly onto the stage, her bare feet barely making a sound on the wooden platform. The music began to swell—a haunting, graceful melody played by a string quartet—and she started to move.

Her movements were fluid, like water, each one melting into the next with such precision that it was hard to believe she wasn't part of the night air itself. Her arms stretched high above her head, and her body followed in a perfect arc. I could feel the power and grace in each leap, each spin, but there was something almost otherworldly about the way she moved—like she was floating rather than dancing.

The music swirled around us, the strings pulling at my heart with their melancholy notes, while the dancers' feet seemed to barely touch the ground, as if they were weightless. The choreography was complex, telling a story that had me leaning forward in my seat, captivated. Each step seemed to carry a deep emotion—longing, joy, pain—and I couldn't help but wonder if there was something the dancer was trying to tell me without speaking a word.

I glanced at Adam out of the corner of my eye. He was watching the stage too, his posture relaxed, but his focus unwavering. There was something about the way he looked at the performance that made me wonder what was going on in his head. His jaw was slightly clenched, but it didn't seem to be in frustration. He seemed to be caught up in the magic of the moment, just like the rest of us.

The first act ended with a slow, sweeping movement—a beautiful, heart-stopping pirouette that left the dancer suspended in midair for just a moment, before she floated down to the stage with an almost imperceptible landing. The audience burst into applause, and I couldn't help but join in, clapping with the rest of the crowd. The dancers had earned every bit of that applause.

I felt a pang of something I couldn't quite identify. The performance had been beautiful, no doubt about it. But sitting there, under the stars, with the warmth of Adam so close beside me, I couldn't stop the thoughts from swirling in my mind. The graceful, almost otherworldly way the dancers moved—it was like they were all chasing something. And I couldn't help but wonder if I, too, was chasing something that I wasn't sure I would ever catch.

The second act began soon after, and the ballet's mood shifted, becoming more playful and joyful. The dancers moved with a lightness that made me smile, the choreography lifting my spirits. But even with the beauty of the performance before me, I felt the weight of the unspoken words between Adam and me, pulling at my attention, distracting me from the show.

I tried to ignore it, focusing instead on the story unfolding on the stage. The dancers twirled and leaped in a vibrant burst of color. Their expressions were so alive, so full of joy and energy, that I couldn't help but feel my heart lighten, just a little.

"Are you enjoying it?" Adam's voice, low and casual, broke through my thoughts. I turned toward him, surprised to find him looking at me with a raised eyebrow.

I smiled, the tension between us momentarily forgotten. "Yeah," I said, watching a pair of dancers perform a synchronized duet. "It's... really beautiful."

Adam nodded, but there was something unreadable in his gaze. He didn't say anything else, but his presence beside me was enough. The music swelled again, the strings rising to a crescendo, and I leaned back into my chair trying to let myself be swept away by the performance.

But as the night stretched on, the ballet's story of love and loss, of joy and heartache, seemed to reflect the turmoil in my own heart. Maybe I wasn't as good at pretending as I had thought. The more I saw the dancers give themselves to their art, the more I felt myself giving in to what was growing between Adam and me.

But no matter how hard I tried to focus on the beauty of the performance, a question lingered in the back of my mind: What if this wasn't just a summer fling?

* * *

The drive back from Sand Harbor was quiet, the night sky stretched out above me, dotted with stars. The sound of the car engine hummed in the background, but it felt like everything around me was muffled. My mind was still wrapped up in the ballet, in the graceful movements of the dancers, and in the heavy silence that had fallen between Adam and me. After driving around for a while, I finally made my way back home.

By the time I pulled up to the house, the porch light was glowing softly in the distance. Sarah's car was already parked in the driveway, and I could see her silhouette through the window as I approached. She must have been waiting up.

I was barely out of the car when Sarah stepped onto the porch, a knowing look on her face. "What did you think of the ballet?" she asked, but her tone was casual enough to hide the fact that she was already reading between the lines.

"It was beautiful," I said, trying to sound upbeat. "Really impressive." I forced a smile, but it felt like it was only skin-deep.

Sarah narrowed her eyes as I walked up the steps to the porch, a slight frown tugging at her lips. "Uh-huh. And everything's okay with you and Adam?"

I froze mid-step, the question catching me off guard. I hadn't expected her to pick up on the tension so quickly, but Sarah was perceptive like that. She always knew when something was off, and tonight I knew she could tell that things weren't quite right between me and Adam.

"What do you mean?" I tried to play it off, but it came out weaker than I'd hoped.

"Please," Sarah said, crossing her arms. "You think I didn't notice? You two were so quiet tonight. Even during the ballet, there was some serious... distance between you." She raised an eyebrow. "So what happened? Did he finally figure out you two were just pretending?"

I winced. Her words hit a little too close to home. "It's not like that," I said quickly, even though I wasn't entirely sure how to explain it. "We're fine. Just... you know, busy."

Sarah studied me for a moment, her eyes softening as if she knew I was trying to avoid the truth. "Rachel, come on. You know you can talk to me, right?"

I sighed, looking out at the darkened lake in the distance. My mind was still swirling with everything that had happened between Adam and me tonight—the ballet, the lingering tension, and his comment earlier about not wanting to just pretend anymore. It wasn't just that he'd said it—it was the way it had made me feel. Real.

"Something happened tonight," I admitted quietly, my voice barely above a whisper. "I don't know... things just feel different now. Between me and Adam."

Sarah's expression softened even more. She stepped closer, her voice gentle. "What do you mean? What happened?"

I hesitated for a moment, but then everything spilled out in a rush. "I don't know. We've been pretending this whole time, you know? But tonight... It was like he was upset, and I could tell he didn't like the way I've been treating this whole thing. He doesn't want it to be fake anymore, and I don't know what to do with that. I don't know what I'm feeling either."

Sarah studied me carefully, as if weighing every word I said. Then she gave a small nod, her eyes understanding. "I get it. You're both figuring it out." She paused, letting the words hang in the air. "But you can't keep pretending forever, Rachel. You're not the only one who's been caught up in this."

I felt a pang of guilt in my chest, but also something else—something I couldn't quite name. "I didn't mean for it to be like this," I said, shaking my head. "But every time I start to think it's just for the summer, something else happens. Like tonight... when we were at the ballet. I kept thinking that maybe... maybe this wasn't so fake after all."

Sarah's smile was knowing, but there was a hint of concern behind it. "You think?"

I nodded slowly. "Yeah. I do."

Sarah didn't say anything at first, just took a step back and leaned against the railing. After a long pause, she spoke again. "Well, I won't tell anyone. But you've got to figure it out, Rachel. Because you can't keep going back and forth with him like this. Either you want it to be real, or you don't. And if you do... maybe you should stop pretending it's not."

I chewed my lip, staring down at my shoes, my thoughts still spinning. It was like everything was shifting beneath me. Was I really ready for this? For whatever this thing with Adam was?

"You're right," I said quietly, looking up at my sister. "I guess I'll have to figure that out."

Sarah grinned, her usual teasing tone creeping back in. "I just hope you don't take too long. You might miss your chance."

I rolled my eyes, but there was a flicker of warmth in my chest at the thought of Adam. "I'll figure it out," I said again, but this time, it didn't feel as uncertain as before.

At least, I hoped not.

* * *

The bell above the door jingled softly as I stepped inside Driftwood Coffee House, the familiar scent of espresso and vanilla syrup wrapping around me like a hug. The place had that cozy, lived-in charm—mismatched mugs hanging on hooks, shelves lined with books and board games, sunlight filtering through gauzy curtains.

Lindsey, the manager, waved at me from behind the counter. “Hey, Rachel! You ready for your first day?”

“As ready as I’ll ever be,” I said with a breathy laugh, adjusting my apron and smoothing my hair back into a ponytail.

She handed me a printed checklist and walked me through the espresso machine, the register, where we kept the oat milk, how to fold the pastry bags so the muffins didn’t get squished. My head was spinning halfway through, but I nodded and took mental notes, determined not to mess up.

The morning rush hit around nine, and I got thrown in with another barista, Liv, who was cheerful and fast-paced. I stumbled a few times—frothed almond milk too long, forgot to ask a guy if he wanted room for cream—but everyone was patient, even the customers. A retired couple asked me where I was from. A teenage girl told me my earrings were cute. A little boy waved to me while eating a chocolate croissant.

By noon, I was covered in coffee grounds and smiling so hard my cheeks hurt.

And then, of course, Adam walked in.

He was in his usual faded jeans and a forest green T-shirt, sunglasses perched on his head, hands shoved casually into his pockets as he stepped in line.

My stomach did a ridiculous flip.

Liv nudged me with a smirk. “Is that your boyfriend?”

I gave her a quick smile. “Something like that.”

When he reached the counter, he leaned forward with that crooked grin that always got me.

“One iced mocha, extra whipped cream,” he said, then added, “and whatever your new barista recommends.”

“I hear she’s still learning,” I teased, already moving to grab a cup.

“Yeah, but I’ve got a good feeling about her.”

I rolled my eyes, laughing, but I couldn't help the warmth spreading through my chest. I handed him his drink with a little extra whipped cream and a heart drawn in Sharpie on the cup.

"You know you're not supposed to flirt with the customers," I said, smirking.

"I'll try to behave," he said, "but no promises."

He stepped to the side, sipping his drink, and I swear he lingered for at least twenty minutes, just watching me work—softly smiling every time I rang someone up or laughed with Liv. Like he was proud. Like he was happy just being there.

By the time my shift ended, I was exhausted, my feet ached, and my apron smelled like espresso—but I couldn't stop smiling.

My summer job had officially begun.

And it already felt a little like home.

10

Adam

I was sitting on the couch at home, flipping through a magazine that I didn't really care about, when I heard a knock at the door. I didn't expect anyone, and after a long day of work, I was ready for some peace and quiet. But when I opened the door, there she was—Rachel, standing on the other side, looking a little nervous but determined.

"Hey," she said, biting her bottom lip like she always did when she was trying to figure something out. "Can I talk to you for a second?"

I raised an eyebrow. "Sure. Come on in." I stepped aside to let her in, my eyes trailing over her like they always did. She was wearing one of those summer dresses she liked, something simple, but she looked effortlessly beautiful.

"Thanks," she said, her voice a little quieter than usual. She walked in and paused for a moment in the living room. "I wanted to ask you something."

I leaned back against the doorframe, crossing my arms. "What's up?"

Rachel hesitated, her eyes flicking around like she was deciding how to phrase it. "So, I was thinking..." She stopped, biting her lip again. "Maybe we could go on a date to the casino."

I blinked, not sure I'd heard her right. "A date?" I repeated, a little slower, just to make sure I wasn't imagining it.

She nodded, her cheeks flushing slightly. "Yeah. I know we've been doing this whole 'fake dating' thing for a while, but... I thought it might be fun if we actually did something a little different. Let loose."

A casino date. Of course, she wanted a casino date. It made sense, considering we were in Tahoe. Everyone came here for the same thing—glitz, glamour, and the chance to win big. But I couldn't help the reluctant smile that tugged at the corner of my mouth.

"You sure you want to go there with me?" I asked, my voice dripping with a teasing tone, though it didn't quite hide the fact that I was more than a little intrigued by the idea. "I've got a feeling I might embarrass you in front of all those fancy gamblers."

She rolled her eyes but didn't back down. "You're not going to embarrass me. I'm serious. I think it'll be fun. Just... you and me."

I hesitated for a moment. Part of me wanted to say no—wanted to remind her that this was still just a game we were playing, that it was all supposed to be fake. But the other part of me, the part that had been paying attention to the way her eyes lit up when she smiled, the way my heart seemed to pick up pace every time she was near, wanted to say yes.

"Alright, fine," I said, giving in with a dramatic sigh. "I'll go with you. But only because you look like you really want to do this."

Rachel grinned, her whole face lighting up at the fact that I agreed. "You're the best."

I nodded slowly, but my thoughts were already racing. A real date. I wasn't sure what that even meant between us anymore. The fake dating was starting to blur into something else, and I didn't know if I was ready to deal with that yet. But at the same time, I didn't want to turn her down. And maybe, just maybe, this would give me some clarity.

"Alright, we'll do this," I said, still unsure of what I was getting myself into, but secretly looking forward to whatever this night would bring. "What time are we going?"

She glanced at her watch, a mischievous glint in her eyes. "How about now?"

I couldn't help but laugh, the tension between us easing just a little. "You really don't waste any time, do you?"

"Not when it comes to dates with you," she teased back, stepping closer, her hand brushing mine as she passed. "Now, come on, let's go win some money."

I watched her head toward the door, my heart thudding in my chest. Maybe it was a casino, but it felt like more than just that. It felt like the beginning of something I hadn't been ready to face.

* * *

The casino was bustling with energy—bright lights, the sound of slot machines, and the laughter and chatter of people throwing away their hard-earned money in the hopes of striking it rich. Rachel and I walked through the entrance, and I could feel the tension that had been building between us all week. It was like the atmosphere of the place had ramped up everything between us, making the air thick with possibility.

Rachel was buzzing with excitement, and I couldn't help but notice how good she looked—her dress simple but perfect, her hair catching the lights as she walked. She'd wanted to look like she was going for something casual, but the way she carried herself made it clear this was anything but.

"So, how does this work?" she asked, glancing over at me with a mischievous smile. "Do you just walk in and start playing, or is there a whole fancy ritual?"

I chuckled, stepping up to the nearest roulette table. "Well, you usually throw your money in first," I said, tossing some cash onto the felt. "Then you pray the dealer doesn't take it all."

Rachel raised an eyebrow, clearly amused. "Sounds like my kind of game."

I grinned back, but it was hard to concentrate. Every time she glanced my way, there was that hint of flirtation in her eyes, a subtle change in the way she tilted her head or brushed her hair behind her ear. She was making a point of keeping close, making little jokes, and every time she laughed, I felt it in my chest. It was a little hard to ignore, especially when I knew all of this—every laugh, every touch—was supposed to be fake. But it didn't feel that way anymore.

After a few rounds of roulette, I noticed Rachel was holding her drink a little differently, swaying slightly as she laughed at something I said. It took me a moment to realize what had happened. The woman who had walked in so confident, teasing me, was starting to show signs of being a little tipsy. I wasn't sure how much she'd had to drink, but it was enough that her cheeks were flushed, and there was that lazy, playful smile on her lips.

"Are you okay?" I asked, glancing at her out of the corner of my eye as she took another sip from her glass. Her gaze was a little softer than before, and there was something else in it, something I couldn't quite place, but it made my pulse quicken.

She leaned toward me, her face only a few inches from mine, and for a split second, I thought she might kiss me. But instead, she just gave me that teasing smile again. "I'm fine," she said, voice just a little slurred, as she poked my chest with her finger. "You know, you're kind of cute when you're not being all broody and serious. I mean, you've got that whole rugged outdoorsman thing going for you, which—" She paused, looking me up and down, letting her eyes linger on me in a way that was definitely more than casual. "—works for me."

I swallowed, a little thrown off by her sudden boldness. "I'm glad my ruggedness is working for you," I said, trying to keep my tone light, but inside, I was reeling a little.

She leaned in closer, her breath warm against my ear. "You know," she whispered, "if we were anywhere else, I'd probably be making all kinds of bad decisions right now."

That hit me like a punch in the gut. My brain screamed fake dating—this isn't real—but her closeness, the teasing, the way she was flirting with me, was starting to blur those lines. I wanted to push her away, remind myself of the rules, but I couldn't. Not when her scent was so close, not when her fingers grazed my arm like that, or when she looked up at me with that slow smile that made my stomach flip.

I forced myself to back up, putting a little distance between us, even though it made me feel like I was walking away from something I really wanted. "Let's get some air," I suggested, trying to clear my head. "You're starting to get a little... tipsy."

Rachel didn't argue. She just grinned and followed me, her arm brushing against mine as we headed for the exit. "Maybe that's the point," she said with a wink. "You're not the only one who can have fun tonight, Adam."

The cool night air hit us as we stepped outside, and I tried to shake off the buzz in my head. I could feel the weight of everything that had happened between us over the last few days, and now, with Rachel more relaxed and playful, it felt like I couldn't ignore it anymore.

She tilted her head, eyeing me. "So, what now? You're gonna keep acting like you're not a little into me after all that?"

I didn't answer right away. Instead, I just watched her, trying to decide if I should admit that the lines between us weren't as clear-cut as I'd made them out to be. But then Rachel, as if reading my mind, raised her eyebrows and laughed, the sound light and carefree.

"You don't have to say it," she teased, nudging my arm. "I know you're not that good at pretending."

I let out a breath, half amused and half frustrated. "Maybe I'm just trying to keep my head straight," I muttered.

Rachel's smile softened, and for a moment, it felt like everything else faded away. It wasn't the alcohol talking, or the playful teasing—it was the real Rachel, the one I was starting to get to know.

And for the first time since we'd started this whole fake thing, I wondered if I was really ready to stop pretending.

* * *

The drive back to her place was quiet at first, the kind of quiet that only existed between two people who knew each other too well and still didn't quite know where the line between pretending and feeling was anymore.

I kept my eyes on the road, hands gripping the steering wheel a little too tight, trying to keep my focus. But Rachel was sitting in the passenger seat, her legs crossed and her elbow resting casually on the door, her fingers drumming softly against the window. Every now and then, I could feel her eyes on me, and it was like a slow burn in my chest—something I didn't quite know how to handle.

"That was fun," she said, breaking the silence with a soft laugh. "I didn't realize you could actually have a good time in a casino. I thought you were all about hiking and fishing and... you know, doing manly things."

I glanced over at her, smirking. "I can be multidimensional, you know."

She turned her head toward me, her eyes glinting with that playful look I'd started to dread. Or maybe I was starting to love it, and that was the problem. "Multi-dimensional, huh?" she teased, shifting in her seat so she was facing me more directly. "I bet you've got a lot of hidden talents I don't know about. Maybe a whole secret life as a high-stakes poker player."

I laughed, trying to push down the heat that was building in my chest. "You're giving me way too much credit."

But Rachel wasn't having it. "Oh, I don't know," she said, leaning closer, her voice low and teasing. "You've been keeping some pretty good secrets. Like how you really feel about me."

I couldn't help but glance at her, catching the way her lips curled up into that knowing smile. It was like she was daring me to respond, daring me to admit that maybe I wasn't as good at pretending as I thought.

I forced a laugh, my eyes still on the road. "What's that supposed to mean?"

She didn't pull back. Instead, she leaned even closer, her breath brushing against my cheek. "It means," she said softly, "that I think you might be a little more into this 'fake dating' thing than you want to admit."

I could feel the warmth of her body just inches from mine, the tension hanging in the air like a thick fog. Her perfume, the light scent of vanilla and jasmine, was overwhelming, and it made it hard to breathe.

I cleared my throat, trying to keep my voice steady. "Yeah, well, you're the one who started all this pretending in the first place," I said, a little more sharply than I intended. "You can't blame me for just playing along."

Rachel leaned back into her seat, but I could still feel her gaze on me, heavy and persistent. "Maybe," she said, drawing out the word, "but I'm starting to wonder if you're really as good at pretending as you think you are."

That hit me harder than I wanted to admit. I shot her a quick look, my heart beating faster than it should have. "What do you mean by that?" I asked, the words coming out more serious than I'd intended.

She didn't answer right away. Instead, she let the silence stretch between us, the tension thickening until it was almost suffocating. Finally, after what felt like an eternity, she spoke again, her voice soft, almost teasing. "I mean that I think maybe you're starting to like this—us. And I don't think it's just the 'fake' part anymore."

I couldn't stop myself from glancing over at her, but I quickly looked away, staring straight ahead at the road. My hands tightened on the wheel. My heart was pounding, and I was struggling to keep my cool.

The truth was, she was right. Somewhere along the way, I'd stopped pretending. Or maybe I hadn't been pretending at all. Maybe I'd just convinced myself I was. But how the hell could I admit that? How could I admit to her—or to myself—that this thing between us was no longer just some game?

I cleared my throat again, trying to shake off the feeling. "You're imagining things," I said, trying to sound dismissive, but the words came out flat. "This is all still part of the plan, right?"

Rachel didn't respond right away. Instead, she just looked at me with those eyes—eyes that seemed to be reading me, peeling away the layers I'd worked so hard to keep intact.

"You keep telling yourself that," she said, her voice soft and steady. "But I think you know the truth."

I didn't say anything in response. I couldn't. The truth was, I didn't want to admit how much I did like this—how much I did like her. Not just the flirty, teasing Rachel, but the one who'd shared real moments with me, the one who had laughed with me until I forgot why I was mad, the one who had kissed me without hesitation and left me wanting more.

We pulled up to her house, and for a moment, neither of us moved. She didn't say anything else, but the silence between us was loud—louder than anything else we'd said all night.

I was half-tempted to reach over, grab her hand, and pull her toward me. But instead, I just sat there, staring ahead at her house, wishing I didn't feel like I was about to do something stupid.

Finally, Rachel broke the silence. "Thanks for tonight," she said, her voice quiet but sincere.

"Yeah," I said, still unable to look at her. "It was fun."

She hesitated for a moment, then reached for the door handle. "Goodnight, Adam."

I nodded, but my voice caught in my throat as she stepped out of the truck. "Night, Turner."

And just like that, she was gone—leaving me alone in the truck, my heart pounding in my chest, and my thoughts a tangled mess.

She was right. I wasn't just pretending anymore. And I had no idea what the hell to do about it.

11

Rachel

The tram ride up to Heavenly Ski Resort was like something straight out of a postcard. I could barely keep my eyes off the view, the lake below shimmering like a sapphire in the sun, and the mountain peaks rising around it. As the tram slowly ascended, I couldn't help but press my face against the glass, trying to drink in every inch of the view. Tahoe already sat at over six thousand feet, but Heavenly sat much higher.

"Not bad, right?" Adam's voice broke through my thoughts, and I looked over at him. He was leaning against the railing, his arms crossed casually as he watched the scenery.

"Not bad? It's incredible," I said, my voice full of awe. "I don't think I've ever seen anything like this before."

He smiled, a little amused. "It's not exactly a hidden secret. A lot of people come up here for the views. Most of them leave with a couple hundred photos."

I snorted. "Yeah, probably. I'm trying to figure out how to get the perfect Instagram shot," I teased, glancing out the window again. "I feel like I need a fancy winter coat or something to look the part."

Adam chuckled, a deep, familiar sound. "You wouldn't be the first to think that. Half the people up here come dressed to impress—whether they're skiing or just posing for photos."

I laughed, shaking my head. "Well, I didn't pack anything fancy. Just me and my hiking boots."

"I think you'll survive just fine," Adam replied, giving me an amused glance as the tram started to slow.

Once we stepped off the tram, the cool mountain air hit me, crisp and refreshing. We started down the trail, winding our way through tall pine trees. The path was rocky and uneven in places, but the more we climbed, the quieter everything seemed. The hustle of the town below, the noise and the chaos, felt miles away. I could see why Adam liked it up here.

"So," I asked, breaking the silence as we walked side by side. "Do you do this kind of thing often? Like, just hike for fun?"

Adam looked over at me, his eyes scanning the trees. "More than I probably should. I like the quiet, the space. It's the one place I can actually get away from everything... except now, apparently, you," he teased, his tone light, but there was something else underneath it, something I wasn't sure I could pinpoint.

I grinned back at him. "Well, maybe I need a break from my version of chaos, too," I said, motioning vaguely down the mountain. "But I'm guessing you have a secret talent for getting people to hike up mountains for fun."

He gave me a sideways look. "You're lucky. I don't usually take people on this kind of stuff. But for some reason, you didn't seem like the kind of person to turn down a challenge."

I laughed. "I'm up for it if you are. Let's see who's in better shape."

"I didn't hear you complaining on the way up," he shot back with a grin.

We kept walking, the trail opening up more the higher we climbed. The pine trees gave way to more rocky terrain, and I could see the lake far below us, glittering in the sunlight. It was surreal up here, like a different world.

After a while, we came to a lookout point—just a small wooden platform with a railing that overlooked the lake. It felt like we were on top of the world, and I couldn't help but stand there for a moment, just taking it all in. The wind was cooler up here, and I felt a chill run through me.

Adam stepped beside me, his gaze sweeping over the lake. "This is what I come for," he said quietly. "You get to the top, and you're rewarded with this. Doesn't hurt that the hike isn't half-bad either."

I nodded, still taking in the view. "I get it now. It's beautiful."

Adam didn't say anything for a moment, just stood there beside me. There was a kind of quiet between us, not uncomfortable, but... something more than just casual. I could feel it in the air, that unspoken connection, but I wasn't sure what to do with it. It wasn't exactly the time to ask. I glanced over at him, trying to catch a glimpse of something behind his expression, but he was focused on the view.

"So what now?" I asked, shattering the moment, but the words came out lighter than I'd intended. "Are we racing back down, or what?"

Adam smirked at me. "Race? Are you sure you want to challenge me?"

"Absolutely," I said, a playful spark in my voice. "Don't think I'm just some beginner who'll get tired halfway down the mountain."

His eyes twinkled with amusement. "Okay, fine. But if you lose, you have to carry me down."

I raised an eyebrow. "Oh, you're so sure you're going to win? That's cute."

He laughed, clearly enjoying the back-and-forth. "I'm just saying, you better start warming up. There's no way you can keep up with me."

I grinned back at him. "Oh, you're going down. I hope you're ready."

We started making our way back down the trail, moving quicker now, the challenge in the air between us. But it wasn't just about the race anymore—it was something else, something that felt like we were learning something new about each other with every step. Something I wasn't sure how to name, but it was definitely there.

* * *

The trail was a bit steeper on the way down, the loose gravel underfoot making each step a little more careful. The air was cooler now, and the sun was starting to dip behind the peaks, casting a soft golden glow over everything.

I glanced over at Adam, who seemed totally at ease, even though he was moving faster than I was. His long legs ate up the ground with ease, and I couldn't help but admire the way he carried himself. He was so effortless, like the mountain was just another part of him, something familiar. It was hard to picture him as anything but this confident guy who seemed at home wherever he went.

"So, do you come up here by yourself a lot?" I asked, trying to break the silence that had settled between us as we descended.

Adam slowed a little, glancing back at me. "Yeah. I guess you could say I'm used to the solitude." He kicked a small rock out of the way, his voice casual, but there was something underneath, like he was measuring his words. "Growing up, I didn't really have a lot of friends, at least not ones I could rely on. So, I learned to enjoy time alone. Hiking, fishing, whatever. It's not a bad way to live, if I'm being honest."

I was quiet for a moment, trying to process his words. I'd always seen Adam as this confident guy, someone who could talk to anyone and never seemed to have a care in the world. But hearing him talk like this—like he didn't always feel like he belonged—was a surprise.

"Is that why you don't bring people up here?" I asked, testing the waters. "Because you like being alone?"

Adam shrugged, but it felt like he was choosing his next words carefully. "It's not so much about being alone. It's more about not needing anyone else to validate me. I guess I've gotten used to doing things for myself."

The way he said it made my chest tighten, and I wondered if there was more to it. "You've always seemed pretty... I don't know, self-assured. Like you don't care about what people think."

He glanced over at me, his eyes softening just a little. "It's a lot easier to pretend you don't care when you don't give people the chance to get close. But yeah, I guess I've been pretty good at faking it."

I didn't know what to say. I wanted to ask more, to push him for more details, but there was something about the way he spoke that made me hesitant. It was like he didn't want to be seen as weak or vulnerable, and I couldn't blame him. I had my own walls, my own ways of shutting people out, and it wasn't easy to let them down.

"I get that," I said quietly, picking up the pace to match his. "I think I've always been good at pretending, too. Like, I never really let people in. Not for a long time."

Adam's gaze lingered on me for a moment before he spoke again. "Yeah? What about now?" He raised an eyebrow, a playful challenge in his voice.

I paused, surprised by his question. It was a simple one, but it felt loaded. Did he want an honest answer? Would he even believe it? I wasn't sure.

"I don't know," I said slowly, glancing up at him. "Maybe it's different with you."

He gave me a small, almost imperceptible smile. "Different, how?"

I shrugged, trying to brush it off. "I don't know. It just is. You make it easy to talk, I guess. And I didn't expect that."

Adam's smile faded a little, but there was still something warmer in his expression. "I don't make it easy. You just let it happen. You're more open than you think."

I felt a strange flutter in my chest at his words, but I wasn't sure what to do with it. Was he being sincere, or was he just being Adam—charming and confident, making everything seem so effortless?

The silence between us stretched, but it wasn't awkward. It was comfortable, like we both understood that sometimes you didn't need to talk to make things feel right.

As we continued down the mountain, I stole a glance at Adam, trying to make sense of what was going on between us. It was like he'd let me in just a little bit, and even though I wasn't sure where that would lead, it felt... good. Safe. And maybe that was enough for now.

"So," I said, shifting the mood with a lighter question, "do you have any big plans after this? Or is it just the usual hiking, fishing, and avoiding the world?"

Adam grinned, the playful side of him returning. "Well, I was thinking about getting some breakfast. A nice, greasy breakfast with eggs and bacon and whatever else is bad for you."

I laughed. "That sounds like exactly what I need after a long hike."

"You're welcome to join me," he teased, nudging me with his shoulder as we reached the base of the trail.

I smiled back, feeling a little more relaxed now that the weight of our earlier conversation had lifted. "I think I'll take you up on that. If it's as good as you're making it sound, it might be just the thing I need to recover from this 'hike.'"

Adam laughed, the sound rich and warm. "You're gonna need it. I'm pretty sure I just kicked your butt on the way down."

I raised an eyebrow. "I don't know about that," I said, but there was no bite in my words. "I might have slowed you down a little on purpose."

"Oh really?" he said, looking over at me with a challenge in his eyes. "You'll never admit it, will you?"

"Nope," I said, shaking my head with a grin. "I'm not that easy to beat."

"Guess we'll have to see about that next time, huh?"

I couldn't help but laugh again. "Next time. Definitely."

As we reached the bottom of the trail and the parking lot where his truck was waiting, I felt a strange mix of emotions. We'd talked more than I expected, and in some ways, I felt like I understood Adam a little better. It wasn't much, but it was a start.

Maybe there was more to this—more to him—than I'd initially realized.

* * *

After a long, winding drive down the mountain, Adam pulled into a small diner that looked like it had been around for decades. The faded neon sign above the door buzzed faintly, casting a soft glow in the early morning light. It was the kind of place where the coffee was strong, the booths were worn in just the right way, and the menu offered everything you could possibly crave after a morning outdoors.

The bell above the door jingled as we walked in, and the waitress, a woman with short gray hair and a bright red apron, greeted us with a warm smile. “Morning, kids! Two for breakfast?”

Adam nodded, a smile on his face as he led me to a corner booth. The kind with the cracked vinyl seats and the slightly sticky tabletop that somehow made everything feel more authentic. I slid in across from him, feeling the faint ache in my legs from the hike, but also a quiet satisfaction from the whole experience.

“Coffee?” the waitress asked, already reaching for the pot.

“Yes, please,” I said, not even bothering to look at the menu yet. I was already imagining a mug of strong, black coffee in my hands.

Adam glanced at me, eyes narrowing playfully. “Strong enough to wake you up?”

“Better be,” I said, glancing around the diner. “I need something to make up for that hike. I think my legs are already going on strike.”

He smirked. "You weren't complaining when we got to the top."

"Give me a few hours," I shot back, crossing my arms. "I'll have a full list of complaints by then."

The waitress poured coffee into our mugs with a practiced hand and left us alone to look at the menu. Adam slid the laminated sheet across the table toward me, his eyes twinkling. "The pancakes here are legendary. You should try them."

I picked it up, pretending to consider my options. "I'm not sure I'm ready to commit to pancakes yet. Maybe just eggs and bacon... simple."

"Simple?" Adam raised an eyebrow, clearly amused. "What's wrong with you today? You're not taking any risks?"

I laughed, feeling the playful back-and-forth flow more easily between us now. "I'm a woman of mystery, Adam. You'll have to work a little harder to figure me out."

He leaned back in the booth, hands behind his head. "Oh, I'm sure I'll figure it out. Might take a few more pancakes, though."

I rolled my eyes, but I could tell he was enjoying the easy banter. "Maybe. But I'm not here for a food challenge. I just want something that won't make me regret this hike."

Adam grinned. "That's what everyone says before they order the pancakes."

The waitress came back just as I was about to make up my mind. "Ready to order?" she asked, giving us both a knowing look.

"I'll have the pancakes," I said with a grin, raising my hand in mock surrender. "You win, Adam. But don't say I didn't warn you."

Adam smirked, leaning back with a sense of satisfaction. "See? I knew it."

He turned to the waitress. "I'll have the same. Pancakes, eggs, bacon, the whole deal. And a side of those hash-browns. I'm starving."

The waitress nodded and headed toward the kitchen, leaving us alone again. I glanced over at Adam, his playful demeanor still in place, but there was something else behind his eyes—something a little quieter, a little more thoughtful.

"So," I started, picking at the edge of my coffee mug. "What was it about this place that made you bring me here?"

Adam shrugged, his hands folded loosely on the table. "It's just... been my go-to for years. You know, after long hikes or days when I need to clear my head, this place has a way of making everything feel normal. Familiar. Like nothing else really matters for a while."

I was quiet for a moment, processing his words. "That's nice," I said softly. "I get it. Sometimes you just need somewhere like that. Somewhere you don't have to think too hard."

"Exactly," Adam said with a slight nod, his gaze flicking out the window for a moment before meeting mine. "I guess it's not a big deal, but... sometimes, it's enough. Just having a place where things are simple."

I nodded, feeling a deeper sense of understanding between us. Maybe it wasn't just the pancakes that had made this place so special for him. Maybe it was the comfort, the familiarity, the sense of peace that it gave him when everything else in his life felt chaotic or uncertain.

"That's good," I said quietly. "You need that. Everyone does."

For a second, we just looked at each other, the weight of the words hanging in the air between us. It wasn't heavy, though. More like we were finally getting on the same page, understanding the other person just a little more.

The waitress returned with our plates, setting them down in front of us with a cheerful smile. "Here you go, kids. Enjoy!"

Adam immediately dug in, grabbing his fork and cutting into his pancakes with a satisfied grin. "Told you. Best in town."

I took a tentative bite of my pancakes, and the sweetness hit me immediately. It wasn't overly rich, but it was the perfect balance, with just the right amount of syrup to make it indulgent without feeling too heavy.

"Oh, wow," I said between bites. "Okay, you were right. These are pretty amazing."

"I told you," he said with a smug look, digging into his own stack. "The secret's in the batter."

I rolled my eyes, but I couldn't help but laugh. It was hard not to, with Adam so pleased with himself. "Well, I guess I'll have to keep coming back if I want to figure out the secret."

He raised his eyebrows, his eyes twinkling. "You never know. I might have to bring you back here a few more times, just to be sure."

I smirked, leaning back in my seat. "You're on."

* * *

The morning sunlight streamed through the wide kitchen windows, painting golden streaks across the wooden table where my laptop sat open. A blank Word document blinked at me, the cursor waiting patiently as if it had all the time in the world. My résumé draft sat minimized in the taskbar, half-finished, half-forgotten.

I took a slow sip of my coffee—cold now, but I didn't really care—and glanced out the window toward the lake. The water shimmered in the distance, peaceful and impossibly still, like nothing in the world could touch it. I envied it a little. It didn't have to make big decisions about the future. It didn't have to figure out what came next.

The cabin was quiet, Sarah and Kyle off on some morning hike, and Adam—well, I wasn't sure where he was. Probably working. Maybe thinking about me. Or maybe not.

I sighed and clicked the document open again. *Rachel Turner – Communications Graduate. Reliable. Creative. Driven.*

Driven. Right.

I'd been so sure of what I wanted. A job in Oregon. My own apartment. A new chapter, fresh start, all that. And yet now, every time I looked at job listings or started crafting cover letters, my mind wandered back to him.

To Adam.

To the way he looked at me when he thought I wasn't watching. The way his hand had lingered on mine during our fake dates, like maybe it wasn't pretend anymore. The way his teasing had shifted from infuriating to something I secretly looked forward to.

The problem was, I didn't know where we stood. Or if I should be standing still at all.

What if I stayed in Tahoe and it didn't work out? What if I left and always wondered what might've been?

I closed the laptop softly, as if that might quiet the thoughts swirling in my head. But they stayed with me. Just like he did.

12

Adam

I pulled up to Rachel's family's house, gravel crunching under the tires as I parked next to a couple of other cars. The lawn was dotted with folding chairs, and the smell of burgers and hot dogs from the grill was enough to make my stomach growl. The sound of distant fireworks could already be heard in the background, even though it was only early afternoon.

"Here we are," Rachel said, sounding like she was bracing herself. She'd been a little quieter than usual ever since we left the truck, and I could tell she was gearing up for the inevitable round of questions her family would throw at us. She glanced at me with a forced smile, wearing a red tank top and white shorts, her hair loosely tied back. She looked good—maybe a little too good for a "fake" relationship.

I raised an eyebrow. "You okay?"

Rachel adjusted her sunglasses, tapping the frames against her forehead nervously. "Yeah. I just—well, they're going to ask a lot of questions, you know?"

I chuckled, easing out of the truck. "What else is new? This is what families do."

She shot me a quick look. "Not mine. They're relentless. And they're going to love you."

I didn't say anything else. I just followed her toward the front door, the sounds of her relatives chatting and laughing growing louder as we walked.

Before we even reached the porch, Rachel's mom was out the door, her arms wide as she wrapped Rachel in a tight hug. "Sweetheart! You made it!" she said, her voice warm and welcoming. She squeezed her daughter and then pulled back to look at me with a grin. "And Adam! We've heard so much about you. It's so nice to see you again."

"Nice to see you too, Mrs. Turner," I said, shaking her hand. "Thanks for having me."

"Oh, we're thrilled to have you here. We're just so happy to see Rachel," she said, pulling her daughter closer. "We've missed you, honey. Come on in!"

As we stepped inside, Rachel's dad was standing in the kitchen, lifting a spatula in greeting as he flipped something on the grill. He grinned when he saw me. "Adam! Good to see you, man. Come grab a burger!"

"Thanks, Mr. Turner," I said, following Rachel to the backyard, where the rest of the family was set up under a big tent. Tables were stacked with potato salad, fruit bowls, and chips, and the grill was smoking with the promise of food. Rachel's younger cousins ran past us, clearly in the middle of some sort of game, while her uncle was already sitting in a lawn chair with a beer in hand.

Rachel's aunt, who I'd known since I was a kid, waved at us from the picnic table. "Well, well, if it isn't little Rachel and Adam. How's everything been? You two still hanging out together after all these years?"

Rachel stiffened for a second, and I could feel the tension in her shoulders. This was a familiar territory for her—being around family who had watched her grow up and had plenty of opinions about her life. They were all used to her hanging out with me back in the day. There were plenty of jokes about how we were always "inseparable," but that wasn't really the case anymore.

"We're doing well," Rachel said, forcing a smile, though I could see the edge of discomfort in her eyes. "It's been great catching up."

Her aunt raised an eyebrow. "You two have really grown up, huh?" She glanced between us, then leaned in closer, lowering her voice. "So, when's the wedding?"

Rachel's eyes went wide for a second, then she quickly recovered, her laugh coming out a little too loud. "Oh, uh... Aunt Maria, we're not—um, not there yet."

The question seemed innocent enough, but I could feel the heat rising in Rachel's cheeks. She shot me a brief glance, like asking me to somehow play along, but I could tell that her nerves were getting the best of her. It wasn't just the questions that were coming—it was the pressure of having her family assume things about us. After all, we hadn't exactly laid out the truth to them. We'd kept it simple: old friends, spending time together.

Rachel's dad joined us with a fresh round of drinks and a plate of burgers. He handed me a beer, his eyes twinkling. "So, Adam, tell us what you've been up to since you left town. You still working that same job?"

I nodded, trying to keep it casual. "Yeah. I'm still with the same job. Nothing fancy."

Rachel's aunt, who had been listening in, shot me a curious look. "So, tell me—what was it like growing up next door to Rachel? Was she as much of a pain back then as she is now?"

I couldn't help but laugh, glancing at Rachel, who was pretending to ignore the conversation. "You have no idea. She used to get me into all kinds of trouble," I said, playfully nudging Rachel's shoulder.

Rachel rolled her eyes but smiled. "And you always dragged me into yours, so don't act like it was one-sided."

Her family laughed, and the atmosphere lightened. It wasn't that I didn't enjoy spending time with them—it just felt like there was an unspoken understanding that Rachel and I were more than we were letting on. They had seen us grow up together, and I could tell they were waiting for the inevitable moment when we'd finally admit to what was happening between us.

The rest of the afternoon passed in a blur of food, drinks, and small talk. I kept my distance from Rachel here and there, letting her have some space to deal with the questions, but I kept finding myself glancing over at her. I don't know why, but seeing her interact with her family—so at ease with them—made me realize how much I was starting to care for her. More than I'd ever planned to.

* * *

The evening had settled in with a cool breeze rolling off the lake, and Rachel and I found ourselves heading toward my family's house for their Fourth of July party. The air was thick with excitement, and the sky was painted in hues of purple and darkening blue. I could already hear the distant sound of music, laughter, and clinking glasses as we approached the front yard, lit by string lights hanging in the trees.

"This is my family's place," I said, giving Rachel a brief glance. "I'm sure you've been here before."

Rachel nodded, her eyes scanning the large backyard where a bonfire was crackling away, surrounded by lawn chairs and blankets. The sounds of our footsteps in the gravel driveway faded into the background as we walked up to the front door. It was strange, being here with Rachel after everything that had happened between us in the past few days.

I hadn't expected to feel so... complicated about this whole thing. But I had to admit that the more time I spent with her, the more I wanted to believe the fake dating could be something more.

My mom was the first to spot us as we entered the house. She waved enthusiastically and made her way over with a big grin. "Well, look who finally showed up! Rachel, honey, it's so good to see you again!"

"Thanks for having me, Mrs. Harrison," Rachel said, giving her a warm hug. She looked at me briefly, then turned back to my mom. "You have a beautiful home."

"Always good to see a familiar face," my mom replied. She pulled Rachel into a side hug and then turned her attention to me. "Adam, take Rachel out to the fire pit! You two need to catch up with the rest of the family."

"Sure thing," I said, giving Rachel a quick look. "You good?"

Rachel offered me a smile, but it was a little strained. "Yeah, I'm fine."

We made our way outside, past the glowing string lights and the makeshift bar, toward the fire pit. My cousins were hanging around, and I waved to them as we passed, leading Rachel to an empty spot by the fire. The heat from the flames felt good against the evening chill, and I grabbed a couple of drinks before handing one to her.

"So," I said, leaning back on a nearby lawn chair, "how's the evening going for you so far?"

Rachel took a sip of her drink, her eyes flicking over to my cousins who were chatting nearby. "It's good," she said, her tone a little softer than usual. "Your family's nice."

"Yeah, they are. They're a bit much, but they mean well," I said with a chuckle. "They've been asking about you. You know, about when we're getting married."

Rachel's eyes widened for a second, and she gave me a quick glance. "What? They're serious?"

I couldn't help but laugh at the way her eyes widened. "You really didn't notice? They're relentless."

She rolled her eyes, though she was smiling. "They were teasing, right?"

"Some of them," I said, watching her closely. I could feel the warmth of the fire flickering on my skin, and my thoughts were scattered. It was hard to focus when she was so close, laughing like she used to, but also... something else.

The night went on, with fireworks being set off in the distance, the loud explosions echoing through the mountains as the sky was illuminated in vibrant colors. I could feel Rachel's gaze shift toward the fireworks, and I stood up, extending my hand toward her.

"Come on, let's go out front for a better view," I said, leading her through the backyard and toward the large lawn at the front. My cousins and aunts and uncles had gathered there, spreading out blankets and seating themselves in a semi-circle as the show started to get better.

The first firework exploded in a shower of reds and blues, lighting up Rachel's face in the glow. I caught her smile in the reflection of the lights, the soft pinks and reds of the firework display dancing in her eyes.

For a moment, there was only the sound of the fireworks, the crackling from the bonfire, and the rhythm of our breaths. My heart beat a little faster as I stood next to her, watching the explosion of color above us.

"I'm glad we did this," Rachel said softly, her voice almost drowned out by the booms in the sky.

"Me too," I said, my gaze lingering on her more than the fireworks themselves. There was a feeling in the pit of my stomach that I couldn't explain, a pull toward her that was becoming harder and harder to ignore.

She looked up at me, and for a brief second, our eyes locked. The air between us felt different, charged. A smile played on her lips, and I knew, without a doubt, that she felt it too.

I leaned in before I could second-guess myself, gently brushing my lips against hers. It was soft at first, almost tentative, but as the fireworks exploded overhead, so did the kiss. It deepened, and in that moment, I realized I didn't want it to end.

When we pulled away, her breath was just as shaky as mine, and her eyes were wide, glimmering in the light of the night. "Adam..." she said, but she didn't finish her sentence.

I just smiled, looking back at the fireworks, but everything seemed quieter now, somehow. It was like the world had paused for just a second—before the next explosion of color filled the sky.

"Yeah," I said softly, not able to stop the smile from tugging at my lips. "Me neither."

* * *

The drive back to Rachel's house was quiet, the soft hum of the truck engine filling the space between us. The weight of the kiss we'd just shared under the fireworks lingered in the air, heavier than I cared to admit. My hands gripped the steering wheel a little tighter than usual, and my mind couldn't seem to settle. Every now and then, I'd glance over at Rachel, but she was staring out the window, her face illuminated by the occasional passing streetlight.

The kiss had felt real—too real. The softness of her lips, the warmth of her body so close to mine... it wasn't just for show. It couldn't have been. Or could it?

I glanced at her again. Her expression was unreadable, a mixture of exhaustion and something else I couldn't quite place. Maybe she was still processing it too.

"So," I said, trying to keep my voice casual, "that was, uh, pretty intense back there, huh?"

Rachel shifted in her seat, her fingers absently tugging at the hem of her shirt. "Yeah," she said softly. "But... you know, it was just for the family, right?"

Just for the family.

The words hit me harder than I expected. Of course, that's what it had been. A way to convince everyone that we were really dating—nothing more. We had both agreed on that from the beginning. It was all just an act, a way to keep our families off our backs. A way to dodge the questions, the teasing, the awkwardness of not having answers.

But the way she said it—like she was trying to convince herself more than me—made the pit in my stomach grow heavier.

"Yeah, right," I muttered, keeping my eyes on the road. But inside, a dozen questions were racing through my head. Was it just for the family? Was that kiss just for show? Or had I... no, it was too soon. It couldn't mean anything more than what we'd agreed upon.

The truck passed through the town's dimly lit streets, and the silence between us stretched out, heavier with each passing second. Rachel had said it was just for the family. That's all it had been, right?

But why did it feel like something more?

I could feel the weight of her gaze now, but I kept my eyes straight ahead, focusing on the road. "So, uh, I guess I'll just drop you off here, then."

Rachel nodded. "Yeah. Thanks for tonight. It was fun."

Fun. Yeah, that's one way to put it. But I couldn't shake the feeling that there was more to it. More to us. It wasn't just the fireworks. It wasn't just the way her smile had lit up when the sky exploded in color. It was something else. Something real. But I wasn't sure if she felt it too, or if she was just playing along with the whole "fake dating" act.

I pulled up to the curb in front of her house, the engine ticking quietly as I put the truck in park. My heart was still racing, my thoughts swirling in a dozen different directions.

Rachel opened the door and paused before getting out. "Adam..."

I looked over at her, meeting her eyes for the first time since the kiss. "Yeah?"

She hesitated for a moment, like she was deciding whether or not to say something, then finally spoke. "I'll see you tomorrow, okay?"

"Yeah," I said, my voice rougher than I expected. "Tomorrow."

She stepped out of the truck, giving me a quick wave before walking up to her front door. As I watched her disappear inside, I sat there for a moment, letting the silence sink in.

Was it just for show? Or was something real starting to grow between us?

I knew I shouldn't let myself get caught up in it. I knew we had a deal. We were pretending. But as I started the truck and drove off into the night, I couldn't shake the feeling that maybe, just maybe, the lines between fake and real were starting to blur.

And I didn't know if I was ready for that.

13

Rachel

The sun was already high in the sky by the time Adam and I met up with Sarah and Kyle at the beach. The warm sand felt good beneath my feet as we walked across the shoreline, the sound of the waves crashing in the distance. I'd been looking forward to this all week—hanging out with my sister and her boyfriend, enjoying the weather, and hopefully getting a good game of volleyball in. But of course, Adam and I had to pretend like everything was normal after last night. And that was harder than I expected.

"Ready to lose?" Adam grinned, tossing me a volleyball as we approached the net. He was already wearing his board shorts, his arms tan from the sun, and his usual cocky smirk firmly in place. I wasn't sure if I was more annoyed or amused by how easily he slipped back into his playful teasing.

"Please," I said, catching the ball and tossing it back to him. "I'm going to crush you guys."

"That's the spirit," Kyle said, already stretching out by the net, a big grin on his face. Sarah was putting on sunscreen nearby, her eyes glancing over at Adam and me, clearly sensing the tension that still hung between us. She raised an eyebrow but didn't comment.

"I'm just here for the fun," Kyle added, looking at Sarah with a wink. She rolled her eyes and handed him the sunscreen, clearly used to his antics.

Adam was stretching now, his movements smooth and easy. I couldn't help but notice how his muscles flexed under his shirt, and I quickly averted my eyes, forcing myself to focus on the game. The last thing I needed was to be distracted by the fact that I could still feel the heat of his kiss from last night, still taste the faint memory of it on my lips.

"Alright, we good to go?" Adam asked, grinning like he was already planning how to beat us.

"Sure," I said, my voice a little more clipped than I intended, but I couldn't help it. The tension from last night was still hanging in the air. He hadn't said much since we'd parted ways at my house, and honestly, I didn't know what to make of it. Was he really just pretending? Was that kiss just some kind of performance for his family? Or was there something more to it?

We divided into teams—Adam and Kyle on one side, Sarah and I on the other. The game started with Sarah serving, and I immediately focused on the ball, letting the competitive part of me take over. The sand beneath my feet was hot, but it didn't bother me as I set myself up to receive Sarah's serve.

"Get ready!" Sarah called out.

I crouched low, ready to make a play. The ball sailed toward me, and I hit it with a quick spike. Adam was there, of course, always in the right spot, his reflexes sharp. He blocked the ball and sent it flying over the net, sending me into a scramble to get it.

"Nice try," he teased as I dove for the ball, feeling the sand stick to my arms and legs.

I shot him a glare, but I couldn't help the grin that tugged at my lips. "You're going down," I shot back.

We volleyed the ball back and forth, Sarah and I giving it our best, but Adam and Kyle were definitely the better team. Every time I tried to make a move, Adam was right there, teasing me in his usual way.

"You're not getting past me," he said with a laugh, as he leaped into the air to block one of my spikes. The competitive banter between us made the game more fun, but it also made it clear how easy it was for him to slip into that confident, almost cocky role.

At one point, the ball bounced off the net and hit me in the face.

"Okay, that was unfair," I muttered, rubbing my nose.

Adam laughed, his eyes lighting up with mischief. "I'd say it was a great play, actually."

I narrowed my eyes at him, but before I could fire back a retort, Sarah and Kyle called a time-out.

"Alright, let's just call it," Kyle said, holding up his hands. "Team Adam wins."

"What? We're not quitting!" I protested. "We still have a chance."

"Not when he's playing like that," Sarah said, grinning. "Seriously, I'm not even sure how he does it."

We all laughed and took a break, sitting on the sand and cooling off with some water. Adam and I both stayed quiet for a few moments, a little awkward in the silence. I glanced at him a few times, wondering if the kiss last night had meant anything to him, or if he was just acting like it had been a normal part of our "fake" relationship.

"So, how are we doing on the whole 'fake dating' front?" Sarah asked, leaning back on her hands as she watched me. Her tone was light, but I could see the curiosity in her eyes.

I shot her a glare. "Really?"

She grinned. "Hey, I'm just trying to get the scoop. It's hard to keep up when you guys are both being so weird about it."

"Nothing to say," I said quickly, looking away. "We're just... keeping it low-key."

"Uh-huh," Sarah said skeptically, raising an eyebrow. "Sure you are."

Adam didn't say anything, but I noticed the way he shifted in the sand, looking away from me. There was a flicker in his eyes, a hint of something I couldn't quite place. Was it annoyance? Frustration? Or maybe something else?

"Let's just finish the game," I said, standing up and brushing the sand off my legs. "I'm not going to let you guys win that easily."

Adam looked at me, a small smile tugging at the corner of his lips. "Bring it on, Turner. You've got a long way to go."

And just like that, the game was back on. I couldn't tell if the tension between us was thickening or if it was starting to fade, but either way, I had to focus. I had to win. But deep down, I couldn't help but wonder if maybe, just maybe, Adam wasn't as interested in pretending anymore as he let on.

* * *

The sound of Sarah and Kyle's laughter echoed through the beach as they grabbed their things and started heading back toward the parking lot. Sarah waved over her shoulder at me, a teasing smile on her face as she mouthed, Good luck. I rolled my eyes but smiled back, grateful for the break from her constant teasing.

Adam and I were left alone on the sand, the sun still high in the sky, but the late afternoon warmth had a more relaxed feel to it now. The beach was quieter, the usual sounds of waves crashing against the shore and the soft murmur of voices fading as the crowd thinned out. It was just us, with a towel laid out beneath us and a cooler full of drinks between us.

I settled down next to the cooler, pulling a bottle of water out and twisting the cap off. Adam had stretched out on the towel, his eyes squinting against the sun. His shirt was already off, revealing his tan and the muscles of his arms and chest, his tattoos running down one arm in a way that made me look away a little too quickly. I didn't know why I felt this sudden pull of attraction every time I looked at him. It wasn't supposed to be like this. This was *fake* dating, wasn't it?

"How's the water?" he asked, glancing over at me.

I took a sip of water and leaned back on the towel, stretching out my legs. "It's nice. Definitely colder than I thought it would be."

He smiled, that easy grin that had been making my heart race for weeks. "Yeah, the lake's always like that. Pretty cold for a place that looks like it should be warm."

"I don't get it," I said, propping myself up on my elbows and glancing over at him. "It's beautiful here. The weather's amazing, the lake's right there, and yet... it always feels like you have to work harder to enjoy it. Like, it's almost too perfect."

Adam laughed, running a hand through his messy hair. "That's because perfect doesn't exist," he said. "You have to appreciate the imperfections. That's what makes it real."

There was a small pause as I took in his words. He'd never been one for deep thoughts, at least not when we were younger, but now... he was different. We both were. This summer had made everything feel more real, even though we kept trying to pretend it wasn't.

"Yeah," I said, my voice quieter. "I guess you're right."

Adam shifted, sitting up and reaching for the bottle of sunscreen next to me. "I need to put some more on before I turn into a lobster," he said, cracking open the bottle. "You're good for now, but I should probably get your back too."

I blinked, a little caught off guard. "You want to put sunscreen on me?"

His grin was mischievous as he uncapped the bottle. "Well, yeah. Unless you want to risk getting burned and being all uncomfortable tomorrow."

I couldn't deny that he had a point. "Fine, but you better not turn this into some weird competition, okay?" I said, lifting an eyebrow at him.

Adam chuckled, a playful twinkle in his eyes. "Would I do that?"

I shot him a look, but I didn't pull away as he moved behind me. He squirted some sunscreen into his hands and began to rub it over my shoulders, his touch surprisingly gentle, almost like he was taking care not to make things more awkward than they already were. It was such a simple gesture—something we'd probably do for a friend—but as his hands moved over my skin, I felt my pulse pick up. My breath caught in my throat for just a second.

His fingers brushed the side of my neck as he worked the sunscreen into my shoulders, and I flinched, surprised by the sudden jolt of warmth that ran through me. He paused for a second, and I could have sworn I heard his breath hitch too. When he spoke, his voice was a little softer, like the moment had changed between us.

"Is it weird?" he asked, still working on my back, his touch steady but with something else in it now. "That we're doing this? Pretending, I mean."

I glanced over my shoulder at him, my heart unexpectedly thudding in my chest. "What do you mean?" I asked, keeping my voice steady.

He hesitated before continuing, his hand brushing a few strands of hair off my shoulder. "I don't know," he said slowly. "Just... sometimes I wonder if maybe this isn't all just for show. If maybe we're not pretending anymore."

My breath hitched at his words, and for a moment, I couldn't speak. My pulse was racing, but I wasn't sure if it was because of his touch or what he'd said.

"You know this is just for the summer, right?" I managed to say, my voice quieter than usual. "Just until I leave. We don't have to make it... anything else."

Adam was silent for a moment, his hand still on my back, and for a second, I thought maybe he hadn't heard me. But then he spoke, his voice low, almost like he was trying to figure something out.

"Yeah," he said, but there was a faint edge to his tone. "I know. But sometimes, I don't know what's real anymore. You and me... it doesn't feel like it's just for show."

I turned to face him then, my heart pounding in my chest. Our faces were closer than I realized, and the air between us felt thick with unspoken words, with questions neither of us had asked.

I opened my mouth to say something, but the words didn't come. Instead, I found myself just staring at him, caught in the warmth of his gaze. For a moment, I almost thought he might kiss me. My body tensed in anticipation, but then he looked away, clearing his throat.

"So, um," he said, rubbing the back of his neck, "are we done with the sunscreen? Or do you want me to get the rest of your back?"

I forced myself to snap out of whatever daze I'd fallen into and stood up, suddenly feeling too exposed. "Yeah, that's fine," I said, trying to laugh it off. "I think I'm good."

Adam looked at me for a beat longer than necessary before he gave a small nod. "Okay. Just making sure."

We both took a step back, the air still crackling between us, but neither of us said anything else for a while. There were so many things I wanted to ask, so many things I wanted to know, but all I could think about was how close we'd been just now—and how much I wanted to stay that way.

But this was supposed to be fake. It was just for the summer.

Right?

* * *

The drive back to my house was quiet, the hum of the truck's engine and the occasional sound of tires on the gravel road filling the space between us. Adam kept his eyes on the road, but I could feel the weight of the silence pressing down, heavy with all the things we hadn't said. I didn't know what to say either, so I kept my thoughts to myself, even though my mind was racing.

I couldn't stop thinking about the way his hands had felt on my skin. It had been so simple, just sunscreen, but the way he'd touched me—it had made my heart beat faster than it should have. And when he'd spoken, when he'd said that maybe this wasn't just for show anymore, something inside me had shifted. The air between us had thickened, and for just a second, I had wondered if maybe, just maybe, he wasn't pretending either.

But I couldn't let myself get carried away by that. This was supposed to be fake. Just a summer fling. A way to make both our families stop asking questions. We'd agreed on that—I'd agreed on that. The rules were simple. No feelings. No strings.

So why did I feel like something was slipping between us, like we were both holding back, afraid to admit what was happening?

I glanced over at Adam, his jaw set in that quiet concentration as he drove, his hands relaxed on the wheel. He looked like he always had—confident, at ease—but there was something different in the way he carried himself now. Something more vulnerable, almost like he was waiting for me to say the next thing, to give him a signal.

"Hey," I said after a long silence, my voice almost too quiet in the cab of the truck. "You, uh, you know this is still just for the summer, right?"

Adam glanced over at me for a brief second, his eyes unreadable. "Yeah," he said, his voice calm, but there was something almost… distant in it. "I know."

But did he?

The words didn't feel as convincing as they should have. In the past, I had said it a million times, and it always felt like a shield, something I could hide behind. But now, with the way he'd touched me, with the way he'd opened up about how it wasn't just for show anymore, it felt like I was the one trying to convince myself. I had been pretending for so long, telling myself that the end of the summer would be easy, that we'd go back to our lives, our separate worlds, and forget about this little experiment.

But what if I didn't want to forget?

What if there was something more than pretending? What if I wasn't ready to say goodbye, to let this go?

The truck bumped gently as we turned onto the road leading up to my house. The familiar driveway came into view, and I felt a pang in my chest. I didn't want this drive to end. I didn't want to step out of the truck and go back to my old life, pretending everything was fine, pretending that the spark between us didn't exist. But I wasn't sure what to do with it either.

I didn't know what I was feeling, and that terrified me.

"Thanks for today," I said, trying to sound casual, like I hadn't been lost in my own thoughts for the past few minutes. "It was fun."

Adam pulled up to the curb and parked the truck, but he didn't immediately get out. He just sat there for a moment, staring out the windshield, and I could feel his eyes on me, though I didn't dare look back at him.

"Yeah," he said after a beat, his voice quieter than usual. "It was fun."

Neither of us made a move to leave. The silence stretched out again, thick with everything we hadn't said. I could feel him holding back, just like I was, both of us too afraid to take the next step.

"Rachel," Adam said finally, turning slightly toward me, his voice low. "You know I'm not pretending, right? That... what's going on between us, it's not just some act for our families. It's not like that for me."

His words hit me like a wave, crashing through all my carefully constructed walls. For the first time, he was being open with me in a way that made my stomach twist in a way I hadn't expected. He wasn't just saying the words to make it easier for both of us. He was saying them because he meant them. And that scared me more than I cared to admit.

I opened my mouth to say something, but the words wouldn't come. I wanted to tell him that I felt the same way, that I had started to think maybe this wasn't just pretend anymore. But I couldn't. I couldn't let myself admit it. Not yet. Because if I did, everything would change. And I wasn't sure I was ready for that.

Instead, I forced a smile and glanced over at him, my heart pounding in my chest. "I think I should go inside."

Adam nodded, his face unreadable, and I saw the brief flash of something in his eyes. Maybe regret. Maybe hope. I couldn't tell.

"Yeah," he said softly. "I'll see you later, Rachel."

I opened the door and stepped out of the truck, the cool evening air hitting my skin. I didn't look back as I walked up the steps to the front door, but I could feel his eyes on me, watching me from the truck. I wasn't sure what was happening between us anymore, but I knew one thing for certain—I couldn't keep pretending forever.

And maybe, just maybe, I didn't want to.

14

Adam

The sun was beginning to dip behind the mountains, casting a warm golden glow over the lake as I pulled the paddle boat out onto the water. Rachel had insisted that she was fine, but I could tell she was still holding something back, like the weight of all the unspoken words between us was pressing down on her too. And I couldn't stop thinking about the way she'd looked at me last night, how I couldn't get the feel of her lips against mine out of my head.

We'd agreed to keep things light, but the more time I spent with her, the more I realized how hard it was to ignore what was happening between us. It wasn't just some silly game or a fake date anymore. I'd been trying to pretend like it was, but every time I was near her, the lines started to blur.

I glanced over at her as we paddled along the lake, her face lit up by the soft, fading light. She was looking out over the crystal clear water, a thoughtful expression on her face, and I couldn't help but wonder if she was feeling the same way I was.

The sound of the water lapping against the boat was the only noise between us for a few moments, and I let the silence stretch, hoping she'd say something. But she didn't. She just kept staring out at the distant shore, her arms resting casually on the side of the boat, like she was trying to look calm, but I could tell she was struggling with whatever was on her mind.

I sighed and shifted in my seat, still paddling as we glided over the water. "You know," I said casually, trying to keep the mood light, "if I had known how much work paddle boating was, I would've chosen something else."

Rachel gave a soft laugh, but it didn't quite reach her eyes. "Yeah, it's not exactly the most relaxing activity."

"No kidding," I replied, grinning. "I feel like I'm going to get a workout just from this."

She gave me a sideways glance, a teasing glint in her eyes. "Well, I think you look good with a little sweat on your brow."

The compliment was almost too casual, like she was just throwing it out there without thinking. But it made my chest tighten, because I could tell it was the first time she'd said something like that to me without it being part of the act. It was real. For the first time, I started to think maybe she wasn't just playing along. Maybe she was starting to feel something, too.

I glanced over at her, trying to gauge her expression, but she wasn't looking at me. She was still focused on the water, her lips pressed into a soft line, like she was working something out in her head.

"Rachel," I said gently, my voice a little more serious than I meant it to be. "What's going on with you? You've been... distant lately."

She flinched, like I'd caught her off guard, and then turned to look at me. Her eyes were wide, like she was searching for something to say, but she didn't speak right away. For a long moment, there was only the sound of the water and the soft creak of the boat.

Then, finally, she spoke. Her voice was quiet, but there was a weight to it that made my chest tighten. "I don't know what I'm doing anymore, Adam."

My heart skipped a beat. I hadn't expected her to say that. I thought she'd deflect, like she always did when things got too real. But instead, she was laying it all out there, just like I had been. And it made my pulse race.

"I don't know if I'm pretending anymore," she said, her eyes meeting mine, and I could see the uncertainty there, the vulnerability that she never let anyone see. "I don't know what this is. What *we* are."

My breath caught in my throat, and for a second, I wasn't sure what to say. I wanted to tell her that I felt the same way, that I was tired of pretending too, but I didn't want to scare her off. I didn't want to push too hard.

"So... you're saying..." I started, trying to keep my voice steady. "You're saying that you don't just want this to be a fake relationship anymore?"

Rachel hesitated for a second, her lips pressed together like she was weighing her words carefully. Then, in a voice so soft I almost missed it, she said, "Yeah. I guess I am."

The boat drifted for a moment, and I felt like I was floating. My heart was pounding in my chest, but there was a part of me that couldn't quite believe it. She really was admitting it—she was admitting what I had been too scared to say out loud. The words hung in the air between us like a fragile promise.

"I've been trying to tell myself it's just for the summer," she continued, her voice a little stronger now, like she was finally letting go of all the walls she'd built up. "But every time I see you, I can't stop thinking that maybe there's something more. And I don't want to lose that, even if it means things are... complicated."

I could feel the grin spreading across my face before I could stop it. She had just opened up to me in a way I hadn't expected, and it felt like everything I had been afraid to admit was suddenly right there between us.

"You're not the only one who feels that way, you know," I said, my voice low and full of conviction. "I've been trying to ignore it, too. But I can't. I don't want to pretend anymore either."

Her eyes widened slightly, like she wasn't sure if she had heard me right. But when I reached over and gently brushed a strand of hair from her face, she smiled—a real smile, not the fake one we had both been wearing for so long.

"That's good to hear," she said, her voice barely above a whisper. "Because I think I'm starting to really care about you, Adam."

And in that moment, with the lake stretching out before us and the soft glow of the setting sun warming my skin, I knew that everything had changed. We weren't pretending anymore. This was real. And for the first time, I felt like I could stop holding back.

I didn't say anything right away. Instead, I just smiled at her, feeling something settle in my chest. It wasn't just for the summer anymore. Whatever this was, it was something that was going to last.

And for the first time, I was okay with that.

* * *

The sun had long since dipped behind the high peaks of the mountains, leaving a soft twilight glow over the lake. The evening air was crisp and cool, but it had the peaceful stillness of a summer night, and everything felt suspended in time. Rachel and I had paddled back to shore, both of us feeling lighter after the conversation we'd just had on the water. She'd admitted she wasn't pretending anymore, and I'd told her the same. For the first time, I wasn't worried about what this—us—meant. I just felt... relieved.

We made our way to the small patch of grass near the water, and Rachel spotted the hammock I'd strung up between two trees earlier in the day. It looked inviting under the soft glow of the lantern I'd lit, the fabric gently swaying in the light breeze. Without a word, she walked toward it and climbed in, the hammock dipping slightly under her weight.

"You coming?" she asked, a playful smile on her face, but her eyes were full of something softer—something real.

I hesitated for a moment. Sharing a hammock felt like a simple thing, but for some reason, it felt like a big step. Maybe it was the way everything between us had changed so quickly, the way our conversations had gone from surface-level jokes to something deeper, more vulnerable. But she looked so comfortable, so open, and I found myself not wanting to pull away from it. Not wanting to pull away from her.

I climbed in beside her, settling against the side of the hammock and trying not to bump into her too much. We both shifted a little, trying to find a comfortable position, and I ended up with my arm stretched out behind her, resting on the fabric. She leaned her head back onto my shoulder, and it felt natural, like we'd always been this way.

There was a quiet moment before either of us said anything, just the sound of the lake in the distance, the soft rustle of leaves in the trees, and the steady rhythm of our breathing. It felt... easy. Uncomplicated. And I found myself wishing it could always be this simple.

"I've never done this before," Rachel said after a while, her voice low but steady. She turned her head slightly to meet my gaze. "I mean, the whole... this—sharing a hammock, just... talking."

I smiled, brushing a strand of hair from her face. "You're not the only one. But I don't mind it. Feels kind of... perfect."

She let out a little laugh, but there was a touch of nervousness in it, a hesitation in her voice. "I've always had a lot of trouble with... this." She gestured between the two of us, but her eyes never left mine. "I think that's why I've always kept people at arm's length. I'm not good at letting people in."

I didn't say anything right away. I wasn't sure what to say. But when I looked at her—really looked at her—I saw the way her jaw tightened, the slight edge to her smile, like she was trying to hold something back.

"Why?" I asked gently. "Why have you kept everyone out?"

Rachel let out a long breath, her shoulders sagging slightly as if the weight of the question had caught her off guard. "I guess I've always been afraid of getting hurt. I saw how people around me changed when they got too close, and I didn't want to be that person. I didn't want to need someone so much that it made everything else feel... fragile."

I nodded slowly, understanding more than she probably realized. I'd seen people get hurt too. Seen how a small crack in a relationship could turn into something irreparable. The kind of thing that made you put walls up, even when you didn't want to.

"I get that," I said quietly. "I've been afraid of the same things. I've always been the kind of person who kept things light, you know? No strings attached. But with you..." I paused, not sure how to put it into words. "It's different."

She was quiet for a long moment, her gaze drifting over the lake, her fingers fidgeting with the hem of her shirt. I could tell she was thinking, weighing everything we had just said to each other, maybe even trying to figure out how she felt. It wasn't easy for either of us, this whole opening up thing.

"You know, I thought this whole 'fake dating' thing would be easy," Rachel said after a while, a soft chuckle in her voice. "I thought I could keep my distance, keep everything in its little box. But it's not like that at all, is it?"

I shook my head, the corners of my lips tugging upward as I looked at her. "No, it's definitely not. I don't know when it happened exactly, but somewhere along the way, I stopped pretending."

Rachel turned her head toward me, her eyes catching mine with a mix of vulnerability and something else I couldn't quite place. "You're okay with that? With... this?"

I smiled softly, letting my hand rest on hers where it rested on her stomach. "Yeah. I think I'm more than okay with it."

She let out a soft breath, and for a moment, she just watched me, like she was searching for something—maybe looking for any sign that I was being honest, that I wasn't going to back out. And I was. I wasn't going anywhere.

"This feels..." she started, trailing off, like she was trying to figure out the right words. "This feels different from everything I've ever known."

"Same," I said. "But I think it's a good kind of different."

Rachel smiled then, that real smile that made my chest tighten in the best possible way. "Yeah, I think it is."

I squeezed her hand, feeling that pull between us again, like we were two pieces of a puzzle finally clicking together. The hammock swayed gently beneath us, the night stretching on around us, and for the first time, I felt like everything was falling into place.

And maybe—just maybe—I wasn't as afraid of it as I had been before.

15

Rachel

The glow of my laptop screen cast a soft light across the cozy living room as I sat cross-legged on the couch, my fingers hovering over the keyboard. The job search tab blinked at me, full of listings in Oregon—entry-level communications roles, marketing assistant positions, a couple of internships I was technically overqualified for but still considering. My résumé was pulled up in another tab, already updated, polished, ready to go.

But I couldn't bring myself to hit send. Not yet.

I stared at the job title in bold font—*Social Media Coordinator, Portland Children's Museum.* It was the kind of job I'd always thought I wanted. Something creative, purposeful, close to home. The idea of going back to Oregon had made so much sense a few months ago. It had felt like a return to familiarity, to structure. To safety.

Now, though…

I leaned back, letting my head rest against the cushion behind me. Through the open window, I could hear the soft rustle of wind through the pine trees, the faint laughter of someone down the road, and the lake's rhythmic lapping in the distance. Lake Tahoe had crept up on me this summer—slowly, quietly—until it wrapped itself around my heart without me realizing.

And then there was Adam.

I closed my eyes and exhaled. His name alone was enough to send a ripple of warmth down my spine. His smile, the way he teased me about my bad volleyball skills, the way he kissed me like he meant every second of it. We had started out pretending, sure, but none of it felt fake anymore. Every moment with him was more real than anything I'd had in a long time.

But that was what scared me.

What if this was just summer magic? What if I stayed, turned down real opportunities, and then we fizzled out? What if I gave up everything I thought I wanted and ended up with nothing?

Or... what if this was everything?

I rubbed a hand over my face and looked back at the job listing. My finger hovered over the trackpad, ready to click.

But I didn't. Not yet.

Because part of me—maybe the braver part—was starting to wonder if love was worth taking a chance on. If maybe, just maybe, the life I thought I wanted couldn't compare to the one that had quietly taken root here.

In this town.

On this lake.

With him.

And I wasn't ready to walk away.

* * *

The morning sun streamed through the kitchen windows as I sat at the table, staring at my half-finished cup of coffee. I was trying to gather my thoughts, but my mind kept drifting back to last night—back to the hammock, to the way Adam had opened up to me, to the way everything felt different now. It was like the line between pretending and real was completely blurred, and I wasn't sure how to navigate it.

But I didn't have long to think about it, because just as I was about to take another sip of coffee, the sound of the front door opening interrupted my thoughts. I turned in my chair, and there was Sarah, stepping into the kitchen with her usual energy. She was wearing a wide grin, like she knew something I didn't. Her eyes darted to me, and she didn't even have to ask—she could tell something was off.

"Hey," she said casually, kicking off her shoes and sliding into the chair across from me. "So... spill. What's going on with you and Adam?"

I froze for a second, my heart skipping a beat. I knew she'd catch on eventually, but I hadn't expected it to be so soon. I thought I'd have more time to figure it out.

"Nothing," I said quickly, but I could tell from the look she was giving me that she wasn't buying it.

"Come on, Rachel," she said, a knowing smile tugging at her lips. "I saw how you two were last night at the beach. You don't just kiss someone like that unless you like them. So, what's going on?"

I shifted uncomfortably in my seat. It wasn't that I didn't want to tell her—it was just that I wasn't sure how to explain it. How could I explain that everything had started as a lie, as something we were both doing just to keep up the act for our families, and now, here I was, wondering if there was something real between us?

"Okay, fine," I said, finally giving in. "It's... complicated."

Sarah raised an eyebrow, leaning forward. "Complicated how?"

I bit my lip, my gaze drifting to the window for a moment as I tried to find the right words. "Well... you know how we were pretending to date, right?" I paused, waiting for her to nod, and then continued. "And at first, I thought it would just be for the summer, just a way to get my family off my back and... whatever. But then, something started to shift. We started spending more time together, talking, doing things that weren't just for show. And I... I don't know. It feels real now. At least, for me."

Sarah's smile softened, and she leaned back in her chair, crossing her arms. "So, you're saying that what started out as fake dating is actually becoming something more? Like, you really like him now?"

I nodded slowly. "Yeah, I guess I do. I don't even know when it happened, but... it's hard to ignore how I feel about him. How he makes me feel."

She was quiet for a moment, and I watched her carefully, trying to gauge her reaction. Finally, she let out a little sigh and leaned forward again, this time with a more serious look on her face.

"Rachel, I'm happy for you. Honestly, I am," she said, her voice softening. "But you've got to be careful. If you're starting to have real feelings for him, and he's starting to feel the same way, then it's not just about keeping up the act anymore. You have to be sure that it's what you both want."

I felt a weight settle in my chest. Sarah was right, of course. I knew that I had to be careful, that I couldn't just jump into something without thinking it through. But every time I was with Adam, everything felt so natural, so right. Maybe it was stupid to ignore it, to keep pretending, but could I really turn my back on something that was becoming real?

"I know," I said, my voice barely above a whisper. "But the thing is, Sarah, I don't want to stop pretending. I don't want this to be just an act anymore. I just... I don't know what happens next. What if I'm wrong? What if I get hurt again?"

Sarah's expression softened, and she reached across the table, placing a hand on mine. "You can't live your life in fear of what might happen. You have to take the leap sometimes, Rach. You won't know if it's real unless you let yourself feel it."

I met her gaze, feeling a lump form in my throat. I'd spent so long building walls, so long keeping people at a distance, that letting myself be vulnerable felt like a terrifying thing. But Sarah was right—sometimes, you had to take risks, even if it meant getting hurt.

"I just don't want to mess it up," I admitted, my voice cracking a little. "I don't want to ruin something that feels... good."

"You won't," she said, her voice steady and reassuring. "You've got this. Just take it one step at a time. And if you like him—really like him—then go for it. Don't let fear hold you back."

I nodded, squeezing her hand in return. "Thanks, Sarah. You're right. I just have to figure out how to let myself feel it."

And maybe that was the first step. Letting myself admit that it was real. Letting myself admit that I wanted this with Adam—not as a lie, but as something that was mine. Something that was ours.

* * *

The evening sky was a canvas of soft pinks, oranges, and purples, as the sun sank lower behind the mountains. The warm breeze coming off the lake carried the scent of saltwater and sand, and the rhythmic sound of the waves against the shore seemed to echo the steady beat of my heart. It was the kind of night that felt timeless, like the world had slowed down just for us.

Adam and I walked side by side along the beach, the sand cool beneath our feet as we moved farther from the crowd. It had been a few days since we'd confessed our feelings to each other, and every moment since then had felt like something new. Real. No pretending anymore. Just us. And for the first time in a while, I felt like I could finally breathe easy.

I glanced up at him, noticing how the fading sunlight caught in his hair, turning it almost golden. His face was soft with a smile, and there was a calmness about him that made my chest tighten with affection.

He caught me looking at him and grinned, that familiar spark in his eyes. "What?" he asked, his voice light.

I shook my head, smiling. "Nothing," I said, but my heart was a little louder than I intended. "Just... happy, I guess."

Adam's smile softened, and he slowed his pace slightly, his hand brushing against mine. It wasn't the first time we'd held hands since we'd started dating, but it still felt new every time. Every touch, every glance, it was like I was seeing him for the first time in a different way. Like everything had shifted.

"You know, I was thinking," he said, his voice low, almost hesitant, like he wasn't sure if I'd agree. "This summer... it's been a lot of things. But mostly, it's been about finding something real. And I want to keep finding that with you."

I stopped walking, turning to face him fully. The words hit me in a way that took me by surprise. It wasn't that I didn't already know how I felt—I had known for a while now—but hearing him say it out loud, so sincerely, made my heart swell.

"I feel the same way," I said, my voice barely above a whisper, as if saying it too loudly might make it all disappear. "It feels real now. More real than anything I've ever felt."

He smiled softly, then reached out, tucking a strand of my hair behind my ear. The simple touch sent a spark through me. "Good," he said, his tone full of warmth. "Because I don't want to go back to pretending either."

We stood there for a moment, just looking at each other, the world around us melting away. It was just us, and it felt like everything was finally falling into place.

"Let's keep walking," I said, my voice a little breathless, and we started moving again, this time more slowly, letting the quiet of the evening settle around us.

As we walked, I felt a growing sense of peace between us, a new kind of intimacy that came with knowing we didn't have to hide anything anymore. We could be ourselves—no more pretending, no more acting.

"So, what's next?" I asked, glancing up at him. "I mean, we've been doing the whole lake life thing, but what else is there for us this summer?"

Adam chuckled, looking down at me with a playful grin. "Well, there's plenty left. We've got all of August. And I still owe you a proper date without any distractions."

I smiled, my stomach fluttering at the thought of spending more time with him, of having the freedom to explore whatever this was between us without any more barriers.

"Then I guess we better make the most of it," I said. "Because I'm not ready for this to end. Not yet."

He gave my hand a gentle squeeze, his thumb brushing over my knuckles. "Me neither."

We continued walking, the golden light of the setting sun reflecting off the water as we neared the edge of the beach. The whole world seemed to stretch out before us, full of possibility. I didn't know what the future would hold, but for the first time in a long time, I was excited for it.

As the sun finally dipped below the horizon, the sky darkening into twilight, Adam pulled me closer, and without a word, we stopped. He looked down at me, his expression soft but intense.

"You know, Rachel," he said, his voice low, almost serious, "I think I've wanted this for a lot longer than I realized."

I met his gaze, my breath catching in my chest. I could feel the weight of his words, how much they meant, how they mirrored everything I'd been feeling.

"Me too," I said softly. "I think we both knew, even when we were pretending. I think we both knew it was real all along."

He smiled, and without another word, he leaned in, his lips capturing mine in a kiss that felt like everything I'd been waiting for. It was slow, deep, and full of promise—real, just like us.

When we finally pulled away, both of us breathless, I rested my forehead against his.

"Yeah," I said with a grin. "Real."

And as we continued our walk along the beach, hand in hand, I realized that this was just the beginning. And I was ready for whatever came next.

* * *

The evening air was crisp as Adam pulled up in his truck to the small, local diner. The neon lights of the sign flickered above us, casting a warm glow on the pavement. It wasn't the fanciest place, but it had a certain charm, and something about it felt just right for our first real date.

I couldn't help but smile as I looked over at Adam. He was wearing a simple shirt and jeans, but there was something about the way he carried himself, the way his eyes sparkled when he looked at me, that made everything feel special. There were no games anymore—no pretending. This was real, and for the first time, I felt like I was right where I was meant to be.

"Ready?" he asked, turning off the engine and glancing over at me with a grin.

I nodded, feeling the flutter in my chest. "Yeah, ready."

We got out of the truck and walked into the diner, the warmth from inside greeting us. The smell of sizzling burgers and fries filled the air, and the sound of soft jazz music played from the speakers overhead. The place was cozy, with booths lined along the walls, and a few locals chatting with the waitress at the counter.

"Two, please," Adam told the hostess, his hand gently brushing mine as we followed her to a corner booth. He slid into one side, and I sat across from him, our knees just barely touching under the table.

"I like this place," I said, glancing around. It wasn't fancy, but there was something comforting about it, something real. "Feels... homey."

Adam smiled, his eyes soft. "Yeah, I thought it'd be good for our first real date. No pressure. Just good food and good company."

I chuckled, not missing the way he glanced at me, his gaze lingering just a little too long. There was something in the way he looked at me now—something different. Something deeper.

We ordered burgers and fries, the easy conversation flowing as we talked about everything and nothing. He told me about a road trip he had taken last year, how he got lost in Oregon, and how he ended up staying at a little bed-and-breakfast for two days because he couldn't find his way out of a forest. I laughed, imagining him wandering around looking frustrated, and he told me that he was pretty sure the innkeeper thought he was a lost tourist.

"I can't believe you got lost in Oregon," I teased, taking a sip of my soda. "You're supposed to be a local. That's like the opposite of a tourist."

"I'm a terrible navigator," he admitted with a grin. "I'll take you on a road trip someday, and we can get lost together. At least we'll be lost in good company."

I smiled at that, warmth spreading through me. "I'd like that."

After dinner, Adam drove us to the local drive-in theater. The large screen was set up in the middle of a sprawling grassy field, the faint sound of cars pulling in echoing in the distance. The night air was cool, and the stars had started to come out, twinkling in the clear sky.

We parked in the middle of the lot, Adam leaning back in his seat and adjusting the radio so the sound of the movie would fill the truck. I couldn't help but smile at how easy this felt. There was no tension, no pretending—just us, together.

He turned to me, that mischievous glint in his eyes. "So, how's your first date going so far? You're not regretting it, are you?"

I laughed, shaking my head. "No way. I'm having a great time."

He looked at me for a long moment, the smile on his lips softening. "I'm glad. Because I think I'm really starting to like you, Rachel. And I don't mean in the 'this is fun' way. I mean in the 'I could totally fall for you' way."

My heart skipped a beat. This was real. And somehow, hearing him say it out loud, made everything feel more solid. Like this wasn't just some summer fling or temporary thing. He really meant it. And I did too.

"I like you too," I said, the words coming easily now. "More than I've ever liked anyone, I think."

Adam's grin stretched across his face, and he reached over to squeeze my hand. "Good. Because I think this might be the start of something pretty damn great."

We settled in as the movie started, the flickering light of the screen illuminating our faces. The film was a classic romantic comedy, and as the night wore on, the warmth between us only grew. We laughed together, shared popcorn, and talked about everything under the stars. But every so often, our hands would brush, and I'd glance over at him, catching the way he was looking at me like I was the only thing in the world that mattered.

When the movie ended, Adam reached over to turn off the truck's engine. The night air felt cooler now, but the warmth between us was undeniable.

"Want to take a walk?" he asked, his voice soft.

I nodded, my heart racing at the idea. "Yeah, I'd love to."

We stepped out of the truck and walked across the field, the distant sound of crickets filling the air. The sky above was a blanket of stars, and everything felt so perfect, like time had slowed down just for us.

"I'm really glad we're doing this," I said, glancing up at him.

Adam smiled, the moonlight catching in his eyes. "Me too."

And as we walked under the stars, hand in hand, I realized that this was it—no more pretending. No more games. This was real. And I was ready to see where it would go.

* * *

The hiss of the espresso machine was practically music to my ears now. I'd figured out the perfect foam-to-coffee ratio for cappuccinos and could ring up three drinks while chatting with a regular and juggling a pastry order—all without breaking a sweat. Well... maybe a little sweat. But still. I was getting good at this.

I wiped my hands on my apron and grinned at the man in front of me.

"Large cold brew, splash of oat milk, two pumps of vanilla," I said, already handing it over.

He looked impressed. "You remembered!"

I shrugged with a smile. "Of course. You're a Tuesday-morning-vanilla-cold-brew guy."

He laughed, handed over a tip, and left with a wave. I rang up the next customer, sliding easily into the rhythm of the day.

Lindsey came over between orders and gave me a small grin. "You're killing it lately, Rachel. I'm really glad we hired you."

"Thanks," I said, a little breathless from the rush but genuinely pleased. "I'm really glad you did, too."

She bumped her shoulder against mine playfully. "There's a full-time position opening up in August. Just saying."

I blinked at her. "Seriously?"

She nodded, then walked away to refill the pastry case, leaving me standing there with that little thrill in my chest.

A few weeks ago, this was supposed to be temporary. Just something to fill the time until summer ended and I figured out what came next. But now... the idea of staying, of really planting roots here, didn't sound so crazy anymore.

When my shift ended, I stepped out into the golden afternoon light and found Adam leaning against his truck in the parking lot, sipping something cold from a to-go cup.

He looked up and smiled when he saw me. "There's my favorite barista."

I walked straight into his arms, pressing my cheek to his chest. "Hey."

He hugged me tight. "You smell like coffee beans and sugar."

"I always smell like that now," I laughed. "Lindsey hinted at a full-time position."

He pulled back just enough to look at me. "That's amazing. Are you thinking about taking it?"

"I don't know," I said slowly. "Maybe. It just... it feels right lately, you know? Like being here makes sense. Like maybe I could stay here while I look for work in my field."

He reached up to brush a strand of hair from my face. "I think Tahoe suits you."

Maybe it did. Maybe *he* did.

And for the first time in a long while, I didn't feel like I was waiting for my real life to begin.

Maybe it had already started. Right here. Coffee-scented apron, lakeside sunsets, and all.

16

Rachel

The sun was just beginning to dip below the horizon, casting a warm orange glow over the water. Adam and I had made our way down to a secluded beach, a hidden spot that neither of us had visited before. It was quiet, the only sound the gentle lap of waves against the shore and the soft rustling of the trees behind us. There were no crowds here, no distractions, just us.

The sand was soft beneath our feet as we walked along the water's edge, the cool evening breeze tugging at our clothes. I could feel the tension between us, that magnetic pull that had only grown stronger since we'd started this real relationship. I glanced over at Adam, his gaze already on me, his expression soft but full of desire.

"Let's go in," he said, his voice low, sending a shiver through me as he stepped into the water. I followed, my feet sinking into the cool sand, the water lapping around my ankles.

The lake was warm, much warmer than I expected, and as I waded in deeper, the water reached up to my knees, then my waist. Adam was close behind me, his presence like a constant pull, drawing me toward him. He reached out, taking my hand in his, the contact electric.

I turned to face him, our bodies just inches apart now, the water swirling around us. There was something about being here, just the two of us, in this quiet, secluded place that felt so intimate. No one around to see, no expectations. It was just us.

"You're beautiful," Adam murmured, his voice barely a whisper above the sound of the waves.

My heart skipped a beat at the sincerity in his eyes. "You're not so bad yourself," I teased, my fingers brushing his arm as I reached up to touch his face.

Before I could say another word, Adam leaned in, his lips capturing mine in a slow, lingering kiss. The world seemed to disappear as I melted into him, the warmth of the water surrounding us, the warmth of his hands on my skin. His kiss deepened, his arms wrapping around my waist as he pulled me closer, the water lapping around our bodies as if it, too, was drawn to us.

I gasped against his lips as he pulled me even closer, my chest pressed to his, the heat of our bodies mixing with the coolness of the lake. I could feel his heart racing, just like mine, the intensity of the moment taking over. The kiss was everything—soft, passionate, and real, everything we'd both been holding back coming to the surface in this quiet, perfect moment.

His hands moved to my back, sliding beneath my shirt, sending a wave of heat through me. I didn't pull away. Instead, I wrapped my arms around his neck, deepening the kiss as I felt the cool water against my skin and the warmth of his touch.

We pulled back for a moment, both of us breathless, our foreheads resting against each other as we caught our breath. The night felt endless, the world outside of this moment fading into nothing.

"I've wanted to do that for a long time," Adam murmured, his voice rough with emotion.

I smiled, my heart pounding in my chest. "Me too," I whispered, before pulling him back to me, kissing him again, this time with everything I felt for him.

The water splashed around us as we kissed, our hearts beating in sync, and for the first time, I didn't feel any hesitation. This was real. This was us.

* * *

The night was clear, the sky a blanket of stars, as Adam and I sat side by side by the campfire we'd built on the beach. The fire crackled and popped, sending little sparks into the air, and the scent of burning wood mixed with the fresh, cool lake breeze. The sound of the waves lapping gently against the shore was the perfect backdrop to our peaceful, intimate moment.

Adam had brought a small cooler with drinks and a few snacks, and I'd found a couple of blankets we could curl up on as we watched the fire. We'd spent the evening laughing, talking, and teasing each other, but now, the warmth of the fire and the calm of the night had settled a peaceful silence between us.

I leaned back against the blanket, pulling my knees to my chest and wrapping my arms around them. The night air was cool, and I shivered slightly, the warmth from the fire offering comfort. Adam seemed to notice, because a moment later, he scooted closer, pulling the blanket over both of us and wrapping his arm around my shoulders.

"Cold?" he asked softly, his voice low, like he didn't want to break the magic of the moment.

"A little," I admitted, feeling a spark of warmth from the way he pulled me closer, his body heat radiating against me.

"You're welcome to steal all my warmth," he teased, his lips brushing my ear as he spoke, sending a shiver down my spine. "I have plenty to share."

I smiled, leaning into him. "Good to know."

We sat in comfortable silence for a while, watching the fire flicker and dance, the flames illuminating our faces in the otherwise dark night. The stars above seemed endless, and the peacefulness of the beach, the fire, and the quiet filled me with a sense of calm I hadn't realized I'd needed.

"I can't believe the summer's almost over," I said, my voice quieter than I intended. It was hard to admit, but I felt the weight of the coming change. I didn't want to leave this place, didn't want to leave Adam. There was something perfect about this moment, something I was afraid would slip away when reality set back in.

Adam shifted beside me, his gaze never leaving the fire. For a long moment, he didn't speak, and I was almost certain he hadn't heard me. But then he spoke, his voice thoughtful, deeper than usual.

"I know," he said, his tone almost wistful. "It feels like we just got started. Like we've only just begun to figure out how good this thing between us could be."

I turned to look at him, and he met my gaze. His eyes, always so intense, softened under the glow of the fire. "I don't want it to end," he said quietly, his hand brushing mine.

My heart skipped a beat, and I felt a rush of emotion flood through me. "Me neither," I whispered, my voice barely a breath. "I don't want it to end either."

He turned to face me more fully, his hand moving to cup my cheek, his touch gentle but firm, like he was making sure I was real. "So, we make it work," he said with a smile. "We figure out how to keep this going, no matter what comes next."

I could feel my chest swell with something—hope, maybe, or fear, or maybe a mix of both. But looking at him, sitting here by the fire under the stars, I knew one thing for sure: this was real. And even though the summer was coming to an end, I wasn't ready to let go of him just yet.

I leaned in, pressing my lips to his, letting the kiss linger, slow and sweet, the firelight dancing in his eyes as he kissed me back. His lips were warm, his touch steady, and the way he held me close made everything feel so right, like I was exactly where I needed to be.

When we finally pulled away, we were both breathless, our foreheads resting together as we shared a quiet moment under the sky. The fire crackled beside us, and the world seemed to fall away, leaving only the two of us—here, in this moment, with the stars above us and the warmth of the fire surrounding us.

"I don't ever want to forget this," I said softly, my voice barely above a whisper.

"You won't have to," Adam replied, his voice steady and sure. "Because I'm not going anywhere. Not this time."

The promise in his words settled deep in my chest, and for the first time in a long while, I felt certain about something. Whatever came next, I wasn't facing it alone.

* * *

After some time by the fire, the night growing chillier, Adam and I finally decided it was time to head back to his place. The drive back was quiet, the only sound between us the hum of the engine and the occasional rustle of the wind through the trees. His hand was warm on the steering wheel, but every now and then, his fingers would brush mine, sending a spark through me.

When we pulled into his driveway, the lights of his cabin spilling out through the windows, he turned to me with a quiet smile. "Want to come in for a bit?" he asked, his voice a little hushed, like he wasn't sure if I would want to.

I felt the pull of the night, the lingering warmth of the fire still inside me, the undeniable connection between us. Without saying anything, I simply nodded. "Yeah, I'd like that."

He gave me a small grin, his eyes warm as he reached over to open the passenger door for me. "Come on, then."

We walked inside, the familiar scent of wood and leather greeting me as we crossed the threshold. It was cozy here—dimly lit with soft, golden light. The walls were decorated with a mix of photographs, souvenirs from his travels, and some of his own artwork. It was the kind of place that felt like home, and I couldn't help but feel comfortable there, the weight of the day lifting as I stepped inside.

"Make yourself at home," Adam said, his tone lighter now as he kicked off his shoes. "I'll grab us a drink."

I sat down on the couch, my fingers absently tracing the stitching on the armrest, my thoughts still swirling from everything that had happened tonight. From the campfire, the fireworks, and the kiss under the stars. The connection we had was undeniable, stronger than anything I'd felt before.

A few minutes later, Adam came back with a couple of beers in hand. He handed one to me before sitting beside me. "I hope this is okay," he said with a teasing smile. "I'm not exactly known for being a perfect host."

I took the bottle and smiled back, trying to keep things light. "It's perfect," I said. "I'm not picky."

We talked for a while, the conversation flowing easily between us. Adam's usual teasing was gone now, replaced by a more serious, quieter side. We talked about our families, our pasts, and where we thought our lives were headed. The more we talked, the more I realized how much I wanted to keep this—whatever this was—going. I wasn't ready for the night to end.

Eventually, the conversation drifted to silence, the kind of comfortable quiet that only happens when two people really know each other. Adam shifted closer, his hand grazing mine, his touch warm and familiar. My breath hitched, and I turned to look at him.

His eyes were on me, dark with something I couldn't name. "Rachel," he whispered, his voice soft, "you've got no idea how much I want you."

Before I could respond, his lips were on mine, the kiss deep and urgent. My heart was racing in my chest, and I could feel the heat between us growing, the world outside of this room slipping away. His hands moved to my waist, pulling me closer as I tangled my fingers in his hair.

The kiss deepened, and I felt the tension between us explode into something electric. Adam stood up, pulling me gently to my feet, and without breaking the kiss, he led me toward the bedroom. The door closed softly behind us, and for a moment, we simply stood there, our bodies pressed together, the air thick with anticipation. Then, finally, he pressed his lips on mine, soft and patient. I knew what this was—what it could be—but there was no stopping it now. I wanted him. There was no hesitation, no doubt.

17

Rachel

The morning after Adam and I shared that quiet, electric moment, I woke up feeling like I was walking on air. The soft morning light filtered through the window, casting a warm glow over the room, but I couldn't shake the feeling that the decisions I'd made were all starting to come together in ways I hadn't expected.

I knew what I had to do. I wasn't ready to leave Tahoe yet, not after everything that had happened between Adam and me. So much had changed in just a few weeks, and it was like the life I had in Oregon was starting to feel like a memory, something that no longer belonged to the person I was now.

I made my way downstairs, trying to shake the lingering thoughts of Adam, but I couldn't. He was everywhere. In the way he held me last night, the way his lips lingered against mine, the way he made me feel like I wasn't just another person to pass through his life. I was someone—someone who mattered.

I crossed over to our cabin, where I found Sarah on the couch, flipping through her phone, her face lit up by the screen. She didn't even look up as I sat down beside her, but I knew she was waiting for me to speak. She always did.

"So," Sarah began, her voice casual but with a little too much knowing in it. "How was last night?"

I felt my cheeks flush, and I looked away quickly, suddenly unsure of how much I wanted to share. But then, she nudged me with her elbow, her grin wide.

"I'm guessing you didn't just come home after the bonfire," she teased, raising an eyebrow. "Did you?"

I sighed, rubbing my hand over my face. "I... I don't even know how to explain it. Everything between Adam feels different now, Sarah. Like, I can't stop thinking about him. And I don't just mean the way he kisses me." I paused, glancing at her, trying to gauge how much I should let her in. "I think I'm falling for him."

Sarah didn't say anything at first, just watching me carefully as I spoke. Finally, she leaned forward, her tone suddenly serious. "Rachel, I think you already know what you want to do."

I met her eyes, my heart pounding. "What do you mean?"

She gave me a knowing smile, her voice softer. "You've been talking about leaving, about going back to Oregon and applying for jobs there, but..." She trailed off, the implication clear in her eyes. "You're not ready to leave, are you?"

I hesitated, unsure of how to answer. I wanted to go back to Oregon, back to the familiar routine, but the thought of leaving Tahoe—leaving Adam—felt like a weight I couldn't carry. "I don't know," I finally admitted, my voice quiet. "I've been thinking about it a lot, and... I'm not sure I'm ready to go back to Oregon yet. Not after everything that's happened here."

Sarah studied me for a long moment, and then she nodded slowly. "I get it. You've found something here. Someone." She grinned at me. "It's not hard to see. You're head over heels."

I looked down, feeling the truth of her words settle inside me. "I think I am," I whispered. "And I don't want to leave him. Not now. Not when everything is... so good. So real."

She gave me a gentle nudge. "Then why don't you stay? Apply for jobs here, Rachel. You've already made a life for yourself here this summer. You're already building something real with Adam. Why go back to Oregon when you've got everything you want right here?"

I bit my lip, the idea of staying in Tahoe slowly starting to feel like the right choice. The thought of applying for jobs here, settling in, and building a life with Adam—with him—was the only thing that felt like it made sense. I didn't know what the future held, but for the first time in a long while, I felt like I had a chance to be happy. To be exactly where I wanted to be.

"I think you're right," I said, finally meeting her gaze. "I'm going to stay. I'm going to apply for jobs here. I don't want to go back to Oregon, not when there's a chance for something real here. For me."

Sarah smiled, a proud and knowing look on her face. "I'm happy for you, Rachel. But just promise me one thing."

"What's that?"

She leaned in, her voice teasing but soft. "Don't let him get away. He's a keeper."

I laughed softly, feeling a warmth spread through me. "I won't. I'm not making the same mistake again."

She nudged me with her shoulder. "Good. Because I can already tell—this summer isn't over for you two."

And as I sat there, my sister's words echoing in my mind, I realized she was right. This summer, this life, wasn't over. Not by a long shot.

* * *

It didn't take long for me to decide—my mind was made up. I wasn't going back to Oregon. I wasn't going to walk away from everything I'd found here. So, after talking to Sarah, I knew what I had to do. I had to tell Adam. I had to tell him that this wasn't just some summer fling anymore. That I was all in.

I drove to his place, my heart racing with anticipation and a little bit of nervousness. As I parked in front of his cabin, I took a deep breath, reminding myself that I had made this decision for me. For us.

I knocked on the door, and it only took a moment before Adam opened it, a lazy grin spreading across his face. He looked effortlessly handsome, his shirt slightly rumpled from the day and his hair still damp from a swim, probably. He leaned against the doorframe, looking at me with that easy confidence that always made my heart flutter.

"Hey, you," he said, his voice warm, eyes lighting up as he stepped aside to let me in. "What's up? You're looking a little serious."

I offered him a half-smile, though my insides were a little jittery. This felt big. Not just telling him my decision, but the decision itself—it was a turning point in a way.

"I have something to tell you," I said as I stepped inside, the familiar scent of wood and coffee filling the air. I stood just inside the door, watching him closely as he closed it behind me, sensing the change in my demeanor.

"Yeah? What's going on?" He walked over to the counter, his hands resting on the edge, his eyes focused on me.

I took a deep breath and walked toward him. "I've been thinking a lot about what comes next," I started, my voice steady but soft. "And I... I don't think I'm ready to leave Tahoe. Not now. Not after everything that's happened."

His brows furrowed slightly, though his expression stayed carefully neutral. "What are you saying?"

"I'm saying I'm going to stay here. I'm going to apply for jobs, make a life here. I don't want to go back to Oregon." I met his gaze, feeling a rush of relief with the words finally out in the open. "I want to be here. With you."

There was a moment of silence, and I could feel the weight of my words hanging in the air between us. Adam's expression shifted, though I couldn't quite place what he was thinking. His eyes softened, and then he gave a small, almost amused smile.

"So, that's it then?" he asked quietly. "You're staying?"

I nodded, suddenly feeling a little unsure. Was I making a huge mistake? "Yeah. I'm staying. I've realized that this—you—are more important to me than anything I was planning back home. I don't want to walk away from what we've got."

A grin tugged at the corner of his mouth, and he pushed away from the counter. He stepped closer to me, the air between us charged with something I hadn't expected—a sense of relief, maybe, or the realization that we were on the same page.

"You sure?" he asked, his voice low. There was something playful in his tone, but his eyes were serious, searching mine.

"Positive," I said. "This is where I want to be. With you."

His grin widened, and before I knew what was happening, he pulled me into his arms, wrapping me in a tight hug. I leaned into him, feeling the weight of the past few days melt away, replaced by the warm certainty of the moment.

"I'm glad," he murmured, his lips brushing my hair. "I was hoping you'd say that."

I smiled against his chest, the sound of his voice grounding me, making everything feel right. "I didn't know how to say it before, but I think I've always known that I belonged here. And I want to see where this goes... with you."

He pulled back slightly, his hands resting on my shoulders as he looked down at me, his gaze filled with something that made my heart race.

"I've got some good news for you, then," he said with a twinkle in his eye.

"Good news?" I raised an eyebrow, intrigued.

"Yeah," he said, his grin wide. "Because I wasn't planning on letting you go anywhere, either."

I couldn't help but laugh softly, the tension from earlier completely gone. "You better not."

And just like that, with everything laid out between us, I knew I had made the right decision. Tahoe wasn't just a place. It was where I was meant to be—with Adam.

* * *

After the conversation with Adam, I felt a sense of calm wash over me. Everything felt more real, more certain. I wasn't just staying in Tahoe for the summer anymore; I was staying for good. I wasn't sure what the future held, but I knew that staying here, with Adam and the life I'd begun to build, was exactly what I needed.

But there was one person I still needed to talk to. My mom. She'd been so supportive of me moving to Tahoe for the summer, and I knew that this news might come as a bit of a surprise to her.

I pulled out my phone, dialing her number as I sat on the couch, the early evening light coming through the window. My fingers tapped nervously against the screen, but I reminded myself that she'd always encouraged me to follow my heart. This was no different.

She answered after two rings. "Hey, sweetheart! How's my girl doing?"

I smiled, hearing the warmth in her voice. "Hey, Mom. I've got something to tell you."

"Uh-oh," she said, laughing lightly. "That sounds serious."

I took a deep breath. "It is. I've decided I'm staying in Tahoe. I'm not going back to Oregon after the summer ends."

There was a pause on the other end of the line, and my stomach fluttered with nervous energy. I knew she wouldn't be angry or upset, but I couldn't help but wonder how she'd take the news.

"Well, that's a bit of a surprise," she said slowly, and I could almost hear her thinking it through. "But honestly, Rachel, if this is what you want, then I'm happy for you. It sounds like you've really found something special there."

I exhaled in relief, my shoulders relaxing. "I have, Mom. I've realized that I'm not ready to leave. I'm going to apply for jobs here and build a life. I'm not walking away from this—not from Adam, not from the life I'm starting here."

I could almost hear her smile through the phone. "I'm glad you're finally making the decision for yourself, honey. You've worked so hard to figure out what you want, and I can tell this is where you belong."

I felt tears well up in my eyes as her words settled over me, her unwavering support making everything feel like it was finally falling into place. "I didn't know how to tell you. I thought you'd be disappointed."

"Sweetheart, I'm not disappointed. I know you've always been independent, and if this is where you want to be, then I'll support you. You deserve to be happy. And if you're happy there with Adam, then that's what matters most."

"Thanks, Mom," I said, my voice thick with emotion. "I really appreciate it. I wasn't sure how to explain everything, but I just know that staying in Tahoe is the right thing. I've grown so much here."

"I can hear it in your voice. You've become your own person, Rachel. And I'm proud of you. So, I guess you're going to make me come visit you in Tahoe now, huh?" She laughed, a teasing tone in her voice.

I smiled, the weight lifting from my chest. "Definitely. I'll have a guest room ready for you whenever you want to come."

"Good. I'll hold you to that. But for now, just promise me you'll take care of yourself. And don't rush things with Adam, alright? Take your time."

"I will," I promised, though I already knew in my heart that we'd both been taking our time. Our connection was real. And it wasn't going anywhere.

"Well, I'm excited for you, sweetheart," she said warmly. "And remember, if you need anything—anything at all—I'm just a phone call away."

"I know, Mom. I love you," I said, my heart full.

"I love you too, Rachel. And good luck. You've got this."

As I ended the call, a sense of peace settled over me. My mom was on board, and more importantly, she believed in me. I had the support I needed to make this leap, to stay in Tahoe and make it my home.

And with that certainty in my heart, I turned my attention back to the life I was building here—with Adam.

-

As Adam parked the truck in front of the little lakeside bistro, I couldn't help but feel a mix of excitement and nerves. The place was perfect—warm string lights strung across the patio, a view of the lake shimmering in the evening light, and the low hum of laughter and conversation drifting through the air. It wasn't flashy or over-the-top, but it felt... us.

Before I could reach for the door handle, Adam was there, pulling it open and offering me his hand with an easy grin. "You ready for this? First real date as an official couple."

I rolled my eyes at his dramatics but took his hand anyway. "You say that like we haven't spent the last two months practically glued at the hip."

He smirked, tugging me gently out of the truck. "Spending time with you isn't the same as doing this properly. Tonight's about making it count."

His words sent a warmth spreading through my chest, and I squeezed his hand as we walked toward the restaurant. The host greeted us with a smile and led us to a small table on the patio, right by the edge where the view of the lake was unobstructed.

"This is... beautiful," I said as I took my seat, the golden light of the setting sun casting everything in a soft glow.

Adam didn't respond right away, and when I looked over, I caught him watching me instead of the view.

"You're beautiful," he said, his voice low and sincere, the teasing edge I'd come to expect nowhere to be found.

Heat rushed to my cheeks, and I laughed to hide how much his words affected me. "You're really laying it on thick tonight, aren't you?"

"Not laying it on if it's true," he replied, his grin returning as he picked up his menu.

Dinner passed in a blur of conversation and laughter. We talked about everything and nothing—my plans for staying in Tahoe, the hikes we wanted to try, even our favorite childhood memories. At one point, he leaned back in his chair and casually threw out, "I bet you can't remember the last time we weren't competing about something."

"Oh, please," I shot back, grinning. "You're just mad that I always win."

He raised an eyebrow. "Always, huh? Pretty bold for someone who just admitted she's terrible at bowling."

I rolled my eyes, throwing a balled-up napkin at him. He caught it with a chuckle, and for a moment, the rest of the world disappeared.

When the check came, Adam didn't even let me reach for my purse.

"Adam," I protested, though I wasn't sure why.

He just shook his head. "Not tonight, Rach. I've got this."

Walking out hand in hand, we stopped by the edge of the lake, the soft ripple of water breaking the silence. Adam looked out over the dark water for a moment before turning to me. "So, did I succeed? Real date, official couple—did it meet your standards?"

I pretended to think, tapping my chin. "It was okay, I guess."

He narrowed his eyes, stepping closer. "Okay? You're really going to say that after I held the door for you and let you have the last bite of dessert?"

I laughed, and before I could come up with a retort, his arms were around me, pulling me close.

"Okay," I whispered, looking up at him, my smile softening. "It was perfect."

"Good," he murmured, leaning down until his forehead rested against mine. "Because I'm planning on a lot more of these."

And as he kissed me there, with the lake stretching endlessly behind us, I knew this was just the beginning.

18

Rachel

Two years had passed since I decided to stay in Tahoe, and every day since then had been a beautiful reminder that I had made the right choice. Adam and I had grown together, our relationship becoming something I never could have imagined when I first arrived in town. The feeling of love between us had deepened, and it was no longer a "summer fling" or a "fake relationship"—it was real, and it was everything I'd ever wanted.

We had moved in together a few months ago, into a little cabin on the edge of the lake, nestled in the trees. It was cozy, perfect for us, and it felt like home every time I walked through the door.

Today was one of those perfect days—sunny, clear, with just enough of a breeze to make the air feel fresh. We were headed up a trail near our cabin, one we'd hiked a hundred times before, but today was different. Today, I could feel the weight of something important in the air. I didn't know what it was, but Adam had been acting a little mysterious all morning.

"So, are you going to tell me where we're going?" I asked as we walked side by side, my hand in his. We had been climbing the switchbacks for about an hour, and the view of the lake was already starting to peek through the trees.

"You'll see when we get there," he said with that same teasing grin I knew so well.

"You're being awfully cryptic today," I said, laughing lightly. "You know I'm not good with surprises."

"You'll like this one," he replied, squeezing my hand as we continued up the trail. "Trust me."

The trail started to narrow as we neared the top, the trees giving way to an open, rocky outcrop. I could see the shimmering blue of Lake Tahoe spread out below us, sparkling in the sunlight. It was breathtaking, as always. But today, the view felt even more special.

We reached the top and stood for a moment, taking in the panorama. The lake stretched out below us, surrounded by the majestic Sierra Nevadas in the distance. It was a scene I never got tired of, but today, it seemed to hold even more significance.

Adam didn't say anything at first. He simply stood beside me, his hand still holding mine. Then, without a word, he dropped to one knee, his eyes never leaving mine.

My breath caught in my throat as realization hit me all at once.

"Rachel," he said, his voice steady but filled with emotion. "From the moment I met you again, all those years ago, I knew my life had changed forever. I knew that I was meant to be with you. You've been my best friend, my love, and my home all at once. I can't imagine a future without you in it."

My heart was pounding in my chest. I couldn't believe this was happening.

"Will you marry me?" he asked, his hand reaching into his pocket and pulling out a small box. Inside was a delicate ring, the diamond catching the sunlight, sparkling brilliantly.

Tears welled up in my eyes as I looked at him, my heart swelling with more love than I thought was possible.

"Yes," I whispered, my voice shaky. "Yes, I will."

The smile that spread across his face was pure joy, and he stood, pulling me into his arms as I laughed, feeling a rush of emotion flood through me. He kissed me, soft and sweet, as the world around us seemed to pause for just a moment, as if everything had led to this perfect, beautiful moment.

"I love you so much," he murmured against my lips.

"I love you," I said, my voice thick with emotion.

We stood there, wrapped in each other's arms, overlooking the lake that had brought us both together, our hearts full of promises for the future.

And I knew, as I stood there with Adam—my best friend, my partner, my love—that this was just the beginning of our forever.

Six years later

It was a typical morning in the house we had made our home—still the cabin by the lake, but now a little more lived-in, a little more cluttered with the joys and messes of family life. The sun was just beginning to peek through the curtains, and the smell of coffee wafted through the kitchen, mingling with the soft hum of a busy morning.

I stood in the hallway, trying to calm my nerves as I buttoned up my daughter's dress. She was so excited—too excited to be nervous about the big day ahead. And I was... well, I was a mess.

"Mommy, I can do it!" Lily, our five-year-old, tugged at the hem of her dress and spun around in a circle, her dark curls bouncing. "Look! I'm ready for kindergarten!"

She had that look about her—the look that reminded me so much of Adam when he was younger: a mixture of confidence and excitement, as though nothing in the world could possibly stand in her way.

I smiled, adjusting the bow in her hair. "You look beautiful, sweetheart. But let me just make sure your shoes are on the right feet."

Lily squirmed, holding out one foot for me to check. "I did it all by myself, Mommy!"

"And you did a great job," I said, leaning down to kiss her on the forehead. "But I'll double-check, just in case."

As I tied her shoes, I heard the sound of footsteps coming down the stairs. Adam appeared in the doorway, his hair a little messy from the morning rush, but his face lit up as he saw Lily.

"Are we ready?" he asked, a wide grin spreading across his face as he leaned against the doorframe.

"I'm ready, Daddy!" Lily announced, raising her arms in the air as though she had already conquered the day. "Mommy's still making sure my shoes are right."

"I'll give you a break, I'm sure they're perfect," Adam said, walking over and scooping her up into his arms. Lily giggled as he spun her around before setting her down again. "You look beautiful, kiddo. Ready for your big day?"

She nodded, bouncing on the balls of her feet. "I'm going to make lots of friends and learn so many things, Daddy. I'm going to be the best kindergartner ever!"

Adam smiled and walked over to me, his hand sliding into mine as we shared a moment of quiet, watching our little girl's excitement.

I squeezed his hand. "I can't believe it's already her first day. It feels like just yesterday she was a baby."

"I know," Adam said, his voice soft but filled with that same love that had never wavered in the years since we met. "It goes by so fast."

The three of us made our way to the kitchen, where the breakfast table was already set, and I could tell that Adam had been the one to make the pancakes. He always made pancakes on the mornings that were extra important—like today.

We sat down together, and as we ate, I felt that familiar warmth of being surrounded by family—the very thing I had dreamed of since I first arrived in Tahoe all those years ago. I thought of how far we had come, how much we had built together.

Work had fallen into place, too. A few months after Lily was born, I was promoted to manager at Driftwood Coffee House. The role came with long mornings, some stress, and way too many inventory spreadsheets—but it also came with a sense of purpose. I loved my team, I loved our regulars, and I loved the life I was building there, one espresso shot at a time.

After breakfast, we gathered our things—packed Lily's backpack with her favorite snacks, double-checked the lunchbox, and made sure her jacket was ready. Then, we piled into the car, Adam driving as Lily chatted excitedly about what her new classroom would be like, what kind of crayons she was going to use, and how she was going to make a new best friend.

As we pulled up to the school, I could feel the butterflies in my stomach—both nervous and proud. Adam reached over and squeezed my hand, offering a comforting smile.

"You okay?" he asked, his voice full of the same tenderness I'd heard from him a thousand times.

"Yeah," I said, blinking back a tear. "I just... I can't believe how fast it all happened. She's growing up so fast."

"She's ready," he said, his voice confident. "And so are we."

We got out of the car and walked with Lily up to the school. As we stood outside the classroom, she took a deep breath and gave us both a look that was both excited and a little nervous.

"You can do it, sweetie," I said, bending down to hug her. "We'll be right here when you get home, okay?"

Lily smiled brightly, her nerves melting away. "Okay! I love you, Mommy. I love you, Daddy!"

"Love you too," Adam said, bending down to kiss her on the cheek. "Have a great day, kiddo."

As we watched her walk into the classroom, hand in hand with her teacher, I felt a wave of pride and emotion. I turned to Adam, my heart full.

"She's amazing," I said, my voice shaky.

"She takes after her mom," he said, his voice soft, his arm around my waist as we stood together, watching Lily disappear into the classroom.

"Yeah," I said, smiling up at him. "She does."

And in that moment, with Adam by my side and our daughter beginning her new adventure, I knew that no matter how many years passed, no matter what life threw at us, we had everything we needed. We had each other. We had this beautiful life we'd built together.

I kissed Adam's cheek, my heart full as we stood there, watching the next chapter unfold before us.

"Ready for the next adventure?" he asked, his arm still around me.

"Always," I said, resting my head on his shoulder.

We may have started off just as childhood enemies, then played pretend after a spontaneous kiss at a bar, but now, with our family, our love, and our future ahead of us, I couldn't imagine life any other way.

About the Author

Alaina Robbins is a self-published romance author who lives in the Pacific Northwest. She considers herself an expert on life in the PNW after being raised in Alaska, Washington, and Oregon. She spent her childhood summers in Lake Tahoe, inspiring her to write a book about her time there. Her previous book is titled "Caught in Alaska."

www.ingramcontent.com/pod-product-compliance
Lightning Source LLC
Jackson TN
JSHW020359310525
85175JS00002B/17

* 9 7 9 8 2 1 8 6 9 1 3 0 1 *